D0544422

J. A. O'Brien worked for Irish Railways after leaving school but went to colle e at twenty to qualify in theoretical radio and electronics. He returned to Ireland af job as a stock clerk in Smithfield to for Eircom for twenty-eight years. Fol ing early retirement, J.A. O'Brien st writing and has written a number of b including *Foul Death* and *Old Bones*

MURDER IN MIND

As acting DI, Andy Lukeson had not
expected to head up a high-profile murder
investigation, but there he is, thrust
forward into the limelight, investigating
the murder of a woman whose death may
be linked to a string of murders long
unsolved. As he struggles to find the killer,
Lukeson's fears of the case going cold
haunt his every waking moment. Can he
get to the heart of the matter before it's
too late?

Books by J. A. O'Brien
Published by The House of Ulverscroft:

PICK UP
OLD BONES
REMAINS FOUND
FOUL DEATH

J. A. O'BRIEN

MURDER IN MIND

Complete and Unabridged

ULVERSCROFT
Leicester

First published in Great Britain in 2010 by
Robert Hale Limited
London

First Large Print Edition
published 2011
by arrangement with
Robert Hale Limited
London

British Library CIP Data

O'Brien, J. A. (James A.)
Murder in mind.
1. Murder- -Investigation- -Fiction.
2. Detective and mystery stories.
3. Large type books.
I. Title
823.9′2–dc22

ISBN 978–1–4448–0933–6

Published by
F. A. Thorpe (Publishing)
Anstey, Leicestershire

Set by Words & Graphics Ltd.
Anstey, Leicestershire
Printed and bound in Great Britain by
T. J. International Ltd., Padstow, Cornwall

This book is printed on acid-free paper

Prologue

Though tipsy, Kate Blake knew that it was unwise, even downright foolhardy, to walk home alone, but a taxi for the short distance she had to travel to her flat would be nearly impossible to procure; perhaps on Monday or a midweek night, but not on a Friday night when taxis could pick and choose and would naturally opt for the longer and more lucrative fares. She had already phoned three companies whose initial enthusiasm soon waned on finding out her destination. 'You could spit as far as Cramer Street from the Coachman's Inn,' the last dispatcher had said, and had added with sneering disparagement, 'The walk will clear your head, darlin'.'

'Come back inside, Kate,' pleaded Nick Clark, the man she had accompanied to the pub.

'Don't want to go back inside,' she responded with stubborn truculence.

'Then I'll see you safely home.'

'I'd rather be seen home by Jack the Ripper! Thank you very much.'

Clark's temper flared. 'Look — '

Blake shrugged off his hold on her arm.

1

'Just piss off, Nick!'

'Heard enough, have you?' Clark barked at the man who had come to the door of the pub, the same man whose actions had started the dispute between Blake and Clark.

'I merely enquired of the lady if she wanted a drink,' said the man.

'Thought you'd get in her knickers for a G&T, did you?'

'Leave it be, Nick,' Kate Blake pleaded, fearful that a brawl was in the offing.

She had had her reservations about accompanying the relentlessly insistent Nick Clark. She should have trusted her instincts and refused — again. Workplace relationships seldom worked, and having been once bitten she should have been twice shy, having had to leave a previous employment because of the stresses of such a relationship. But her acceptance, she'd hoped, would relieve some of the boiler-house atmosphere which Clark's constant pursuit had built up, and with him about to be promoted to section manager in her section, he could make life very difficult for her. Despite all the hoo-ha about things being better in the work place for women, nothing much had changed — the office wolf was still prowling, unchecked. Complain and there would be a lot of huff and puff, but in the end nothing would be done. A little light

2

wrist slapping, the complainant would move on, and the wolf would be free to roam again.

'Are you siding with him?' Clark ranted.

'No. I just don't want any trouble, Nick.'

Kate Blake walked away, overcompensating, and thereby making her progress all the more erratic. Clark grabbed her arm. 'Don't be daft,' he scolded her. 'How far do you think you'll get before some horny old fart,' he shot the man standing in the pub door a contemptuous look, 'will have you? I'll see you home.'

'You?' she scoffed. 'You're the horniest old fart of the lot.'

'Sod it!' Exasperated, Clark stormed back into the pub. 'You can have the slag, mate.'

'Far to go, have you?' enquired the man, who had tried to cut inside Nick Clark when he had gone to the loo.

'Just the other side of the park,' she replied. 'That's why I couldn't get a cab. Too short a fare.'

'Might I make the same offer, to see you safely home?'

'Cheeky. You're a trier, I'll give you that. The answer's the same. You can both get stuffed.'

'You wouldn't care to join me now for that drink I offered earlier, I suppose?'

Kate Blake almost relented. He wasn't bad

looking, if a tad more worn than he should be at his age, which she reckoned was early to mid-thirties, behind the forties wrinkles. 'It's getting late. Another time, perhaps?'

'Just passing through, I'm afraid.'

'That is a pity.'

'I agree. Safe home then. A word of advice. Don't waste your time. You can do a whole lot better than the man you were with.'

'Very nice of you to say so.'

'It's the truth.'

'Goodnight.'

'Night.'

A short distance on, Kate Blake changed her mind. She would have that drink after all, and sod Nick Clark. She turned, smiling, but the man was going back inside. 'Well, my refusal can't have bothered him that much,' she said. She was about to call out to bring his attention to the scarf which had fallen from round his neck, but she changed her mind.

From the moment she had accepted Nick Clark's invitation, issued a hundred times and refused a hundred times, to 'have a quick scoop', she had been at a loss to understand why she had agreed to accompany him, seeing that she had always considered him to be nothing more than a self-opinionated nuisance with a view of his own worth that was self-delusory. And her opinion was not exclusive. Most of the staff, male and female, at Top Hat Insurance shared her opinion of Clark.

'I wouldn't sneeze germs on him, Kate,' one of her colleagues, Sylvia Crane, had said, just before she had joined Clark for that 'quick scoop'. Crane hinted that Clark had a dark side. It had come to Kate's mind to ask her how she knew, but Sylvia Crane said, 'So they say.' The proverbial 'they', whoever 'they' were.

'Just a quick drink,' Kate said.

'Just be careful,' Crane cautioned, and flitted into a loo cubicle, putting herself out of bounds for further questions.

Kate had been undecided about the neutrality of Sylvia Crane's supposed good advice. Sour grapes, perhaps? The answer would be given shortly after by Clark.

On leaving the loo, Kate looked to the door at the end of the hall that would allow her to reach the rear of the building and the car park, from where she could vanish into the night and think over the weekend about the excuse she would give Clark on Monday morning. Or perhaps she should just simply tell him that she had changed her mind and leave it at that. But that might not be the wisest thing to do, if she wanted to advance her career. Nick Clark might be the office lech, but that did not take from his standing in a business sense, and were he to decide that she was not a suitable Top Hat employee, she'd be out on her ear. The company were good employers, paid more than the going rate and sick benefits, if not abused, were excellent, with free employee motor and life insurance after two years' satisfactory service which she would have in a couple of weeks. And she'd hate having to start all over again, having to go through at least three interviews for the most junior position. Besides, she had made up her mind to study for a professional insurance qualification with a view to promotion within Top Hat or, she dreamed, starting up her own brokerage. All a long way off, of course. But upsetting Clark could put it off for longer still, if not for ever.

'Thinking of doing a runner, eh?'

Startled, Kate swung round on Clark guiltily. 'Don't be daft, Nick.'

'Liar,' he stated flatly.

There was a note of *spoiled child* pique in his voice, and in the flash of anger in his cold grey eyes. She had never before noticed how cold and dispassionate Nick Clark's eyes were. But perhaps it was the strip lighting he was directly under that made him look . . .

Menacing.

The description had singularly forced its way into Kate Blake's mind.

Menacing?

A bit strong, that. She dismissed the notion as fanciful. But then the strip lighting would have nothing to do with his tone of voice.

'Well, actually — '

Sylvia Crane came from the loo, coming up short on seeing Clark.

'Ah, I see,' he said. 'Sylvia's been filling your head with nonsense. Telling you how you shouldn't trust old Nick Clark, right? A woman scorned. Isn't that so, Sylvia, my love. Can't get it through that bimbo skull of yours that I don't go out with slags, can you, darling.'

Sylvia Crane burst into tears and rushed off.

'That was nasty and needless,' Kate said.

'But true. Now that the cow's bad-mouthing of me has been explained, are we still on for that drink?'

'Yes, we are,' Kate replied, angry at Sylvia Crane's charade of concerned friend, when all she had been trying to do was sow doubt in the mind of what she had obviously seen as a competitor.

Walking along the hall, Clark asked, 'Give you the standard warning, did she?'

'And what would that be?'

7

'Oh, dear,' Clark intoned. 'So you're not taking me home?'

'Didn't plan to,' Kate answered honestly.

'Not going to be grateful then?' There was no humour in his laughter.

'Since when did a quick drink become a weekend in the sack?'

'That bitch has done a real number on me, hasn't she,' Clark stated, his mouth mean and narrow. 'I'm not the big bad wolf, you know.'

'Why don't we just have that drink for now, Nick. OK?'

'Fine,' he'd said, with an indifferent shrug.

Surprisingly, the next hour and a half had been pleasantly spent until *the incident*. 'Push off, or you're headed for A and E,' a very belligerent Clark had warned the man who had tried to move in on his territory. It was all down hill after that.

★ ★ ★

The full moon was getting smaller and going further away until soon it became a pinprick of dirty yellow light as the scarf tightened round Kate Blake's neck. She clutched at the scarf, relentlessly squeezing the life from her, in a desperate but futile attempt to ease its crushing tightness.

'Whore! Dirty filthy whore!' said the male

8

voice, distorted and coming from afar, his breath hot on her neck as he pressed against her, groaning.

Kate Blake looked to the moon, a lover's moon she had thought only moments before as she made her way across the park, but it was no longer there. It might have fallen from the sky. It was so dark. Weakness flooded through her. She stopped struggling and welcomed the limpness, which was rather pleasurable, that quickly followed.

1

Sally Speckle woke with a start, trembling with the intensity of her dream. So intense had her dream been that its ripples of pleasure still ran unimpeded through her. She thought: God, but you're a bit old for that kind of dream.

There had been a waterfall in her dream, which she now disappointingly realized was the shower in the bathroom next door to her bedroom. Simon Ambrose, naked, followed her out of her dream, so vibrantly alive and real that she could not help herself checking the other side of the bed for the presence of the man who had seduced her in reality a long time ago, the man who had been her lover for three hectic and mind-blowing months when she had been at Uni.

He began to sing 'Heart Break Hotel', the Presley classic, hopelessly out of tune to the point of it being hilariously comedic. Speckle's grin was bitter-sweet. Memories good and bad flooded back, of the many madcap moments she and Simon Ambrose had shared and, also, the many close, intimate hours during which she had mapped out their future all the way to a golden sunset many years distant. Only to find that it was the stuff of self-delusion when, out of the blue, he upped and left to set up house with a mutual friend.

Some friend, Sally had thought at the time, and in the intervening years her opinion of Sharon Lesley had not changed. She still thought of her as a conniving bitch who had befriended her to steal Simon away, despite her protests to the contrary, backed up by Simon's exhortations of: 'It just happened. These things do, Sal.'

'Don't call me that!' she had responded.

The figurine she had grabbed from the mantel had disappointingly whizzed past the right side of Simon Ambrose's head to shatter against the door of the flat through which he was trying to retreat, pyjamas and trainers in hand, the only items of clothing he had managed to retrieve on a secret visit to the flat, rumbled by her unexpected return from a lecture which had been cancelled.

She hated being called Sal. Sally, she had never been too fond of, but Sal made her sound like a gangster's goodtime gal. And yet, as she now recalled, she had not objected too much when Simon had called her that in the heat of passion, in the still moments of the night. In fact, the abbreviation had had all the charm of a secret pet name — the kind of silly thing that lovers indulged in and which, with hindsight, seemed bloody ridiculous for two grown adults. But then, being in love was all about silly things, really, wasn't it.

She lay back, her eyes gritty with the grunge of poor sleep. A dull throb behind her eyes made her squeeze them tightly shut in an attempt to alleviate the steady thump which started deep inside her head and ended in flashes of piercing bright light.

Migraine.

Lord, she had not suffered a migrane for . . . ? Oh, yes. Not since the day that Simon Ambrose had turned out not to be the god she thought he was, but was instead a man with feet of clay.

She turned away from the dagger of sunlight that flashed through the narrow opening in the curtains to the darker side of the bed where, before she got up, she enjoyed a couple of girlishly dreamy moments that took her back three days to where she had stopped off to partake of lunch on her way back from a meeting of senior officers in Brigham which was convenient to personnel from three divisions and which was considered to be as neutral a venue as was possible for feuding officers to meet.

The meeting had been a bad-tempered

13

affair with each side blaming the other for several cases in disputed borderline areas (all unsolved and no one willing to carry the can) on the fuzzy fringes of divisional boundaries, and with all sides stubbornly holding on to the titbits of information they had acquired (hoping to eventually take the credit for solving the case) which, if pooled, might see some villains behind bars. But, like most other organizations, the police were in the main career driven, and upwardly mobile officers kept an ever watchful eye on the next rung of the ladder, a situation which often permitted a villain to remain free for longer than he or she had a right to, had cooperation rather than entrenchment and personal ambition been the order of the day, and a sharing of information prevailed. The general information (the kind that went to make up form) was, of course, meticulously documented. But the titbits, wherein often lay the clue that made sense of all that had gone before, were jealously guarded.

Within fifteen minutes of the meeting beginning, the initial goodwill had faded and the battle lines, which the meeting had been convened to overcome, were firmly and even more resolutely drawn. The Chief Super drafted in to sort matters out, was quickly drawn into the dispute and soon decided that with less than a year to go to pension, he was not going to bring a great deal of trouble on his head after almost thirty years of going out of his way to chart a middle course between rival factions with no small amount of success. There was talk of a promotion (probably just talk, but one never knew) with a considerable hike in pension and, being only too aware of how much very senior officers despised boat rockers, he was not going to rock the boat. He would draft a report that would flatter the senior officers present, and place the blame firmly and squarely on their more junior colleagues for the lack of progress, and the warring factions would retreat to their respective encampments with mutterings about trying again when the other divisions were of a more reasonable and cooperative frame of mind. Before that happened, promotions would have been secured, pensions got intact, the odd gong awarded, and a biography or two on the best sellers list. And the blame for the lack of progress in apprehending the nasties would have been placed squarely on the shoulders of the foot soldiers. Generals never really lost a war. It was always the lazy foot soldier who got it wrong.

A typical bullshit ending to yet another farce reached, Sally Speckle had cried off with a headache when an adjournment to another more neutral boozer for a mending of fences exercise was agreed. Having rather definitive views as to how the police should get their act together, she was in no mood, leaving was much preferable to listening to the kind of bitching that would go on, on the wings of such a gathering.

'Won't give a toss!' had been CS Frank 'Sermon' Doyle's opinion of the chief superintendent chosen to chair the meeting. 'He's been watching his ass for thirty years. He isn't suddenly going to throw caution to the wind, is he?' He pointed to the ceiling to indicate higher authority. 'And they know that. Handpicked. It'll all be a load of old cobblers.'

No one had contradicted Doyle.

★　★　★

Sally Speckle was on her third spoonful of a very passable mixed vegetable soup at the pub she had decided to stop at for lunch on the way back to Loston when: 'Good God! It is you!' She looked up at the man who was standing at her table, grinning like the proverbial Cheshire cat. 'You haven't changed one iota, Sally,' he said.

Sally Speckle was stunned and excited in

about equal measure.

'Good grief! I haven't become that decrepit, have I?' He chuckled. 'I'll settle for moderately shagged.'

'Simon,' she greeted him with soft reflection, the layers of time rolling back.

Simon Ambrose was much paler and looked a deal older than his thirty-two years. This was the man who, at one time, her world had revolved round. The man she had shared good times with in a cramped flat, when she had been twenty. Only ten years previously, but it seemed an age ago now.

'You,' he said, in his deep bass voice, as rich as liquid chocolate, 'my darling, look stunningly wonderful.'

The rich melodic voice which at one time had held her enthralled had not changed. In the ten years since she had last heard it, it had become even more melodic and entrancing. Or was that simply the way *she* heard it.

'May I?' Taking Sally's approval for granted, Simon Ambrose pulled out a chair, reversed it and straddled it cowboy style in the same way he used to, his chin in his hands looking at her. He even had the same *little boy lost* expression in his eyes which had in the past swept away any dissatisfaction she might have had with him. 'We're still not at daggers drawn, are we?'

'No, Simon.' She said his name softly, enraptured again by the roguish man she had once so deeply and passionately loved.

'Had me worried there for a minute,' he'd said. 'Thought I was about to get my marching orders.'

Sally Speckle recalled the fury which would have had her cut his throat had she got the opportunity on that frightful night of betrayal ten years previously. A rainy November evening, the flat filled with the aroma of the meal she was preparing, hoping that the power would hold out and that the flat's decrepit fuse box would not overload and spoil the meal and her surprise. Lights out after the meal would be okay, though. The power held out, but the meal had been spoiled anyway when, two hours after Simon had been due home, she turned off the cooker, somehow instinctively knowing like all lovers do at the end of an affair, that he would not be coming back. He had phoned three days later to break the news that he had moved in with Sharon Lesley. She had had enough warnings from friends about Sharon Lesley's true intentions towards Simon Ambrose, but she had (as the foolishly blind always do) not listened, so certain had she been of Simon's love and loyalty. Of course, she'd been by far too smug for her own good.

'Please understand, Sally,' he had pleaded. 'Neither Sharon or I would have wanted it this way. These things happen.'

Back then, she recalled, she had been of a mind to beg. But later she was thankful that she had not, and had simply said, 'Of course they do, Simon,' and had hung up, grateful that she had managed to hold back her tears and anger for the couple of moments that the phone call had lasted.

Now, out of the clear blue sky, Simon Ambrose was back in her life and she could not make up her mind whether she liked or hated that. However, there was no denying the resurgence of the old feelings. She would not have imagined it possible, but it seemed that she still had feelings for him and, though they were in no way as intense as they had been, they were certainly not insignificant either.

'How have you been?' he had enquired conversationally, as one might of an old friend with whom he'd lost contact, effortlessly bridging the gap of years.

'Fine,' she replied, and thought: right up to this moment, that is.

'You've still got that kink in your hair you worked so hard to get rid of when we were . . . ' His blue eyes sought a point beyond her as his voice trailed off.

'Not for the want of trying,' Sally said, laughing.

'You mean you're still as much in to hairdressers as you had been? Always wondered what it was about hairdressers and you. Of course, you're hair was always your crowning glory.'

It had not made much difference when he had dumped her for Sharon Lesley, whose hair had been short and mousy. Maybe Sharon had been better in bed, more adventurous. Maybe if she had been more adventurous. But she had always been on the more conservative side of the sexual spectrum. On the other hand, Sharon Lesley (rumour had it) was of a more exotic and *try anything once* nature.

Sally had wanted to ask Simon about Sharon: if they were still together, but she curbed her curiosity. It was all a long time ago, and best left in the past where it belonged.

He held his head sideways, looking at her.

'Not sure I like it short, though,' he said. 'I think I preferred it shoulder length.'

'Just had my thirtieth birthday, Simon. Not a sweet young thing any more.'

'Don't be daft. You haven't changed a day in — '

'Ten years and two months.'

God. Why had she been so precise. It sounded as if she had counted every minute. But her preciseness revealed to her how important Simon Ambrose had been to her all those years ago.

'Not quite,' he said. 'Ten years. Two months. Three weeks.' He trapped her eyes with his, the way he always could, leaving her unable to look away. 'Obviously, you haven't missed me as much as I've missed you, Sally. I miss the old days.'

The invitation to revisit times past was on the table. Sally heard herself say, as if it were a stranger speaking, 'Let's leave the past where it belongs, Simon. In the past.'

'You're right, of course,' he said, apparently not unduly perturbed, much to her disappointment, by her rejection of his invitation. 'The past is never the same reheated, is it.'

Reheated.

Could one find a more unattractive word to describe what had happened between them? But she supposed she was glad. Because had he gone into charm mode which, she knew, could be devastatingly seductive, she might have been drawn once again into the fantasy world she had lived in all those years ago, before she had learned that Simon Ambrose was, above all else, one of life's survivors, utterly pragmatic in the pursuit of his own

21

comforts and desires.

'Drink?' he offered.

'Driving.'

'You always were a cautious one.'

'That sounds like a criticism?'

'Lord, no,' he quickly assured her. 'A compliment, believe me.'

She had believed him once before, and had been made a fool of. She was not of a mind to believe him again. And as he had said, and she agreed, the past reheated was never the same.

'Did you do as well as you'd wanted to in maths?' he enquired.

'Yes.'

'So you're a teacher?'

'No. I'm a police officer.'

'A copper!' The effect of her announcement seemed to have had a startling effect on him, and yet she wasn't at all sure that he was startled. She recalled his ability as a consummate liar and actor who could, with little effort, make anyone believe anything. 'I'd have never had you down to be a copper, Sally.'

'Neither would I have.'

'Then how — '

'I joined the police through the Graduate Entrants Programme, tinkered about with computers and statistics for years, and then one day I was made a detective inspector for reasons that I have not yet been able to fathom out.'

'A good copper, are you?'

'I hope so.'

He pulled at his lower lip. 'Wait a minute. DI Sally Speckle. There was an Inspector Speckle in charge of that case where a load of old bones were found in some wood or other last year.[1] You?'

'Me,' Speckle confirmed.

'There was a doctor involved, wasn't there?' He clicked his fingers. 'Blackman. That was his name, right? Murdered several women, didn't he?'

'Not sure how many. Liked to keep his secrets, Blackman.'

'Came on police radar by chance during the investigation of another murder, as I recall. Picked up a lot of plaudits for that, and your other cases.'

'I've been very lucky with the team of officers who assist me.'

Other cases? Had Simon Ambrose been keeping tabs on her?

'Ever ready to spread the glory around, eh,' he said. 'Never grabbing it all for yourself. Credit where credit is due, right.'

---

[1] See: *Oldbones*

'Of course.'

'So typical. Come to think of it, weren't you the inspector who solved the murder of a woman found on the banks of the Loston river, also?[1] Making quite a reputation for yourself, eh. You always were superefficient, Sally.'

The thought about Simon Ambrose keeping tabs on her returned. It was a ridiculous idea, of course. But there was no denying that he was knowledgeable about her career.

She checked her watch. 'Sorry, Simon. I'm running late as it is.'

'Dumping me, are you?'

'No.'

'After the way I behaved, I deserve dumping.'

'Look, it was all a long time ago, Simon. We've both moved on,' she'd said.

But had she? Had Simon Ambrose's betrayal been the impediment to any meaningful relationship since? She couldn't help wonder. Had she, in fact, a fear of commitment, for fear of it ending so disastrously as it had before? Was that the reason that, at thirty, she had still not settled down and had put her career before any emotional ties?

---

[1] See: *Remains Found*

'Water under the bridge, eh,' he said, with a hangdog look.

Sally had wanted to say, 'Well, maybe not,' to leave the door open until she had got to grips with what her feelings for Simon Ambrose really were. Instead she stood up to leave and said, 'Nice meeting you again, Simon. But — '

'You're running late,' he said soulfully, making her uncomfortable with the lie she had told. She had the entire afternoon and evening ahead of her, with little to do. Quick as he always had been to sense her guilt, even the guilt of a little white lie, he'd said, 'Prove it.'

'Prove what?'

'That you're not dumping me, of course.'

'Don't be ridiculous, Simon.'

'Take me home with you, Sally.'

'Take you ho— ?'

'Yes. It would do my ego no end of good.'

'I'm sure, as always, your ego is perfectly fine, Simon. What're you doing here, anyway?'

'Writing an article, one of a series about English pubs.' Sally Speckle could not hide her surprise. 'For an insignificant Midlands magazine with a circulation of two, the owner and his wife. This is number fifteen.'

Simon Ambrose held Speckle's gaze.

'Not quite the stuff of Booker and Nobel Prizes, Sally,' he said sadly.

'You were a fantastic writer, Simon. Oodles of promise.'

'I quickly realized that the distance between promise and achievement, in my case at any rate, was too far. So now I write articles and bits and pieces. Really any bit of doggerel that'll keep body and soul together. But don't pity me, for God's sake. I can get pissed for nothing. Every pub hoping that I'll write them up in a flattering light. Take this one. The toilets stink and the beer is flat.' Speckle's tummy did a turn. 'But for a free bed and a couple of quid on the side, I've sung its praises.'

'A bit dishonest, that, Simon.'

'Yes, it is,' he conceded, unabashed. 'But it was that or starve for the next couple of days.' He flung back the yellow wool scarf he was wearing; she remembered that he had a thing about scarves, seldom going without one even in mild weather. 'Don't be too critical, Sally. Needs must, and all of that.'

'OK, but you can only stay a day or two,' she found herself saying. She scribbled her address on a page from her notebook. 'I'll expect you when?'

'Tomorrow.'

'Fine.'

'Afternoon.' He held up his half empty glass of beer. 'Late afternoon, probably.'

'Give me a call at work first.'

'Loston nick?'

'Yes,' she said, frowning. 'You have been keeping tabs on me, haven't you,' she added, strangely uncomfortable with the idea.

'Just an interest in an old lover's progress, Sally.'

'I'll expect you then.'

He wrapped the flowing yellow scarf round him with the swagger of an actor exiting his scene, and raised his glass. 'To times past, Sal.'

On leaving, she began to regret her invitation to Simon Ambrose, while at the same time looking forward to having him around, briefly though, for the inevitable trip down memory lane. Time and overindulgence had not been kind to Simon Ambrose but, though his spectacular handsomeness had faded somewhat, he had lost none of his devastating charm, and she had to admit that his dissipated look added a certain character to his face that had not previously been there. It was now what would be described as a *lived in* face.

'Drive carefully,' he called after her, as she drove away. 'Looking forward to a good old chinwag, Sally.'

It had been a week, and Simon Ambrose was still her guest and, worryingly, becoming something of a fixture that she was not too concerned about; in fact, she was beginning to think that when he left, she would probably miss him. However, having thought long and hard about it before she had fallen asleep, she had resolved that today would be the day in which she would tell him that he had overstayed his welcome. And having stumbled into the flat last night, very late and the worse for wear, her resolve to move Simon Ambrose out and return to the well ordered life she had had before she had invited him to stay was absolute. And now that the shower had stopped and he would have returned to his bedroom to get dressed, was as good a time as any to raise the subject of his leaving. Donning her dressing gown, she went and opened her bedroom door and came up short on seeing Ambrose, stark naked, crossing the landing. The sight of him naked sent an electric shock through her: a very familiar electric shock and, had he seen her and beckoned, she had no doubt at all that she would have come panting. She closed her bedroom door quickly and went and sat on the edge of the bed, her emotions racing off in all sorts of directions, one thought uppermost in her mind.

Was she still in love with Simon Ambrose? Or was it just something much more basic?

★   ★   ★

Six-year-old Lucy Burnett stood looking at the woman on the ground, lying on her side, the way she cuddled up to go to sleep. Funny place to be asleep, though, she thought. She'd have to go round the woman to retrieve the ball she had followed into the bushes. She hoped the woman would not wake up. Picking up the ball, she looked behind her at the sleeping woman, her gaze held by the woman's contorted face and the swollen tongue protruding from her open mouth.

2

Chief Superintendent Frank 'Sermon' Doyle looked at Sally Speckle with the asperity with which a host would a gatecrasher at a posh do.

'Sorry,' she apologized. 'Traffic.'

'You seem to have an unfortunate knack of getting into traffic jams, Inspector.'

Sally Speckle shrugged. What else was there to do by way of response to Assistant Chief Constable Alice Mulgrave's *pull the other leg* observation. Doyle's frown deepened. The relatively new ACC[1] had proven herself to be a formidable force in the short time since she had taken up her post, and Doyle had no wish to get on the wrong side of her. Or rather be put on the wrong side of her by Speckle's persistent late attendance at meetings Mulgrave had summoned her to. Speckle was one of those people from whom, despite her best efforts, time constantly slipped away. Time stretched out before her until, suddenly, that spare half hour she had planned on had dwindled away to minutes

---

[1] See *Foul Death*

and the race to beat the clock was on. DS Andy Lukeson had once offered the opinion that her lateness was down to a pathological intolerance of what she saw as a waste of good police time when she could be out chasing and catching villains, doing, as she put it *real police work*, rather than sitting around trying to resolve issues which needed direction from the brass rather than, as she saw it, the brass spreading the muck as wide as possible so, should the time come, collective action or lack of same could be blamed for unresolved issues.

'Too many bloody meetings, Andy,' she had opined, more than once. 'If everyone sits around in offices for the greater part of every day gabbing, who'll be out there to do the real policing!'

'On the other hand, if everyone is gadding about half-cocked, the cure could be worse than the illness, couldn't it,' Lukeson had responded.

'I suppose,' Speckle had conceded grudgingly. 'Maybe I'm just not a team player.'

'Rubbish! You're the most team-orientated DI round here.'

She laughed. 'Oh, God. You mean I'm really a Wilfred Little and not Batman?'

'Wilfred Little?' Lukeson had questioned.

'A lecturer I once had, who organized every

lecture with the meticulousness of a general going into battle, and who constantly waffled on about good preparation being the oil of the machine of perfection.'

'The ACC has a very busy schedule, DI Speckle,' Doyle said gruffly, pointedly checking the imitation Rolex he had picked up at the Saturday Market on Grey's Quay. 'To be waiting around for you to — ' Alice Mulgrave placed a hand on Frank Doyle's arm to curb his rebuke.

'The traffic is rather sticky,' Andy Lukeson said, in Speckle's defence, a defence she would have appreciated at another time, but not when Mulgrave's restraint of Doyle had drawn a line under the matter.

'You got here on time, Lukeson,' Doyle said curtly, in answer to his defence of Speckle.

'I live closer, on a less congested route, sir.'

CS Frank Doyle's eyes were already flashing round the other officers present. 'As did everyone else,' he said gruffly.

'Perhaps it would be best to get on with the business on hand, Chief Superintendent,' Alice Mulgrave said, obviously not appreciating him going on with his rant when she had indicated otherwise. The brief, thorny silence which ensued was used by those present to shift chairs and shuffle papers. Many hooded looks were cast Sally Speckle's way to express displeasure with her. Now it seemed that a routine meeting might turn into an aggro fest.

Frank Doyle's thunderous look at Sally Speckle left her in no doubt as to where he was placing the blame.

The meeting consisted of Loston's entire compliment of senior officers and Acting DI Andy Lukeson, who bravely enquired of Mulgrave: 'May I ask, ma'am, what this distinguished gathering has been assembled for?'

'Do you include yourself among the distinguished, Acting Inspector Lukeson?'

'In my book an Acting DI is as good as a DI, ma'am,' Lukeson said. 'Otherwise what would be the point?'

'Indeed, Mr Lukeson,' Mulgrave said, favouring him with a wry smile.

Lukeson had been appointed to fill the vacancy left by DI Jack Porter who, after a coronary, would be absent for some time if, in fact, being only two years away from pension, he ever resumed duty. It had come as a shock to Sally Speckle that she should lose her sergeant and more importantly a colleague and a friend so suddenly. DC Charlie Johnson had stepped into Lukeson's shoes, put there by Frank Doyle to prevent a repeat of an earlier contentious occasion, when she might again have chosen DC Helen Rochester as Lukeson's replacement.

'Don't want any more handbags, Speckle,' Doyle had said, pre-empting her objection about being sidelined in the decision-making process. 'Johnson has the time in and deserves his chance.'

Time in. Doyle had shown his well-known preference for tradition. She would not condemn him for that. However, hers was a more pragmatic approach of horses for courses, rather than right by time served, because in her experience to date she had learned that some officers were naturals, whereas others were plodders who'd never show the flashes of deductive brilliance or spontaneous initiative that solved cases. Give her innovators any day instead of cogs in wheels — time servers.

'Don't be such a firecracker, Speckle,' Doyle had said, obviously reading her thoughts. 'When you're getting a bit long in the police tooth, you'll probably be like the rest of us with time in and pension not too far off, an enthusiastic advocate of steady as she goes.'

'Sir,' she had replied, with the obedience of a nun to her Mother Superior.

'Now,' Mulgrave said, bringing the meeting

to order, 'I've called you all together to discuss my reorganization plans.'

'Reorganization plans, ma'am?' Lukeson queried.

'Yes, Inspector Lukeson. My reorganization plans,' she stated emphatically.

'I don't see much wrong with what we've got right now,' he spiritedly opined, or cheekily, depending on one's perspective and position on the ladder.

'One never does see anything wrong with what one is cozy with,' Mulgrave replied. 'And therein lie the seeds of complacency which, in my opinion, Lukeson, is the enemy of the effective and efficient administration of the force.'

Andy Lukeson seemed of a mind to take the bit between his teeth, but a kick on the ankle by a colleague sitting next to him, and Frank Doyle's frost-laden expression, brought him up short, but far from satisfied.

'Well, Lukeson?' Mulgrave pressed, acting the bitch in Sally Speckle's opinion by not letting sleeping dogs lie. 'You seemed to be about to say something.'

Andy Lukeson smiled limply.

'Shall we press on then,' the ACC said, checking her watch. 'I've got other meetings.' Her gaze swept the assembled officers. 'It seems that divisional inter-rivalry may be impeding the successful conclusion of some outstanding matters which,' her gaze swept the gathering, 'might be resolved with a little cooperation. 'I do hope that, by the end of my series of . . . chats, everyone from the most junior to the most senior in the divisions will understand that I have no tolerance of vested interests!'

'New broom and all that,' an officer to the back of the room said in an aside to a colleague.

'A new broom that will sweep all those who see the job as a rest home right out the door, DI Rogers!' Mulgrave said curtly.

Stunned that she had heard him, Rogers said, 'Sorry, ma'am.' And meeting Doyle's hostile glare, added meekly, 'Sir.'

'We have an understanding then?'

A collective mumbled 'yes' was returned.

'Then let's crack on with what needs to be done!' Alice Mulgrave said.

★ ★ ★

'Police. There's a woman . . . a dead woman.'

'Can I have your name please, madam?'

'Mel Burnett. In the park . . . Layman's Park.'

'Please remain where you are. An officer will be with you presently, madam.'

ACC Alice Mulgrave said, against mounting opposition to her reorganization plans. 'We need to streamline our operations. Policing is like any other business. There comes a time when procedures have to be changed to take in to account new circumstances.'

'Begging your pardon, ma'am,' DI Jack Alldyce said. 'I can't agree that policing is like any other business. We're not making soap powder or biscuits, are we.'

'And your point is?' Mulgrave asked.

Obviously, judging by his sudden discomfiture under the ACC's stare, Alldyce wished he had curbed his annoyance which had led to his impulsive reaction. However, now that he had challenged Mulgrave, he had been left with two options, the first of which was to maintain his stance, and the second was to slink away.

Neither option appealed to him.

'Well, what I mean ma'am, is that if you're making soap powder or biscuits you have parameters that are set, haven't you. X machines and X workers will produce X product. That's not the way with police work. We can't order up what happens, and therefore we must have enough officers on duty at all times to cope with the unexpected.'

'The unexpected,' Mulgrave intoned. 'Such a mercurial concept. You see, Inspector, the unexpected has no fixed boundaries, and therefore let us say that we had X officers on duty now just in case the unexpected happened and it did not, we'd have too many on duty. And then, later, the unexpected happens, due to the fact that we had too many on earlier, we'd have too few then.

'That's where organization comes in, to use our resources, human, technological and budgetary, to best possible advantage. That way, if and when the unexpected comes along, at all times there will be a reasonable number of officers to meet the challenge.

'Seems right, don't you think?'

She let her gaze drift across the gathering.

'Don't you agree?' she pressed.

Having seen Alldyce sink without trace, no one was of a mind to join him. He looked to his colleagues who stared back like cows looking over a ditch at passers-by. His expression said: *Thanks a bunch.*

Mulgrave went on: 'With the inevitable pressure, resulting from the mayhem that's beset the global financial system in this year of 2009, mayhem that will have far-reaching restrictions into the future, it's inevitable that with so many demands on the Exchequer, sharp budget cuts all round will be the order of the day for some time to come. And it seems sensible that we ready ourselves to deal with the new reality, to provide the best possible service to the public.'

'Seems sensible to me, ma'am,' Doyle said, defiantly staring down those officers present of longstanding service who saw his support for Alice Mulgrave as treasonable. 'What is it that you have in mind, ma'am?'

'High-premium attendances need to be cut back,' she said bluntly. 'New technology is now doing a lot of the labour-intensive work which was the lot of former police officers and, updated, it can even lessen the burden further. So the acquirement of new technology is all-important. Our computer system is, as these things go, past it and is buckling under what is required of it in modern policing. Frankly, police work has become increasingly intelligence driven, requiring less of a presence in numbers. And, whether we like it or not, that's the way it's going to be in the future. So resources will need to be redirected.'

'More boffins and less plods, eh,' Alldyce said, with a quick flash of his eyes at Sally Speckle, who had entered the police by way of the Graduate Entrants Programme, officers who were disparagingly referred to as *graddies* by the traditionalists.

'In a nutshell, Alldyce,' the ACC said. 'But,

of course, there'll always be a need for police officers in the flesh, too. I prefer to think of a future that will combine the best of technology and personnel.'

'Sounds to me that it's the end of the road for more traditional policing, ma'am.'

Alice Mulgrave held DI Alldyce's gaze, and to his credit he did not flinch. 'Things move on,' she said. 'Times change. We must change too, Inspector. Nothing remains the same forever.'

The phone on Doyle's desk rang to break the tension which had crept steadily upwards. For the Chief Superintendent the interruption was welcome. It would give everyone, especially Alldyce who could be a stubborn sod, time to step back from the precipice. 'Yes?' he growled, and listened. It was a brief conversation, lasting only seconds. He hung up. 'A woman's body has been found in Layman's Park,' he announced.

'Park,' Alldyce grunted. 'Nothing more than a patch of scrub.'

'It still has a body on it, Alldyce!' Doyle snarled. 'And the police will want to know why that is, won't they.' His gaze swept the assembled DIs before coming to rest on Andy Lukeson. 'Something to cut your teeth on, Lukeson, I reckon,' he said.

'Me?' Lukeson queried, in as close to a yelp as didn't matter, stunned to be handed a murder investigation on his second day as a DI — an Acting DI at that.

'Have you a problem with that, Inspector?' Alice Mulgrave enquired quietly.

'I would have thought that a murder investigation would be assigned to a senior colleague, ma'am,' he said.

'You're a DI now, Lukeson,' Doyle said.

'Not fully fledged, sir.'

'You can always revert to a DS, Lukeson,' Doyle said ominously. 'That is, if you think you're not up to the job.'

'Oh, I'm up to the job all right sir,' Andy Lukeson responded positively. 'It's just that I don't want to put any noses out of joint.'

Frank 'Sermon' Doyle said determinedly, 'Oh, don't you worry about that, Lukeson. Any nose out of joint, I'll quickly put back in place. Now be on your way.'

'Sir.'

'Good luck, Andy,' Sally Speckle said as he went past.

He grinned. 'Permission to consult?'

She returned his grin. 'My door is always open.'

'Now!' All attention was back on Doyle. 'Can we get back to the business on hand, I'll bring you up to speed later, Lukeson,' he promised.

'I can't bloody wait,' Lukeson murmured, as he closed the door of Doyle's office behind him.

3

The morning was grey with a sky that promised rain before long but, Lukeson hoped, not before SOCO had a chance to make at least an initial examination of the murder scene. With trace evidence now so central to a trial, Lukeson sometimes marvelled at how any crimes were solved in England with rain, and it's damaging effect on scenes of crime, never far away.

It was sometime into his drive to Layman's Park when he realized what the root cause of his unease was that he was missing working with Sally Speckle. He'd have never thought that there was such a difference between being a sidekick and the one carrying the can if success in catching the killer eluded him. And though he had been only a short time in his new role, people, old friends, were distancing themselves from him, not in an outright way but in a more diplomatic fashion, obviously becoming aware of his probable elevation in rank. The police were an insular lot, with very definite lines of demarcation that were a positive deterrent to friendships existing beyond changes in status.

It was, in fact, a very *them and us* organization. He hated the idea of rank being a barrier to the continuation of former friendships, but accepted the inevitability that the force was a club with clubs within, exclusive membership of one ruling out membership of the other. In general, the class structure was on the slide, but the police was a bastion of its former glory, if glory was the right word to describe something that for the few had been a life of privilege, but for the many a life of disadvantage, and often one of utter humiliation.

⋆   ⋆   ⋆

Arriving at the scene of crime, PC Phil Larkin came forward to meet him. 'Hello, Sarge,' Larkin greeted, in his usual familiarly friendly manner which, recalling Lukeson's present rung on the ladder, he quickly amended: 'Sir.'

Lukeson bristled, and enquired brusquely, 'What have we got?'

'A woman. Late twenties to early thirties. In the middle of that lot over there.' He pointed to the clutch of bushes where the woman's body had been discovered. 'Out of the way place, relative to the rest of the park. Like one of those bits of old road left behind when the new one is re-routed,' Phil Larkin observed.

Observing a tracery of new paths being laid, Lukeson thought Larkin's description an apt one. Lukeson went to the edge of the crime scene to test a theory, but saw no signs of the kind of disturbance which would have been present had the murdered woman been dragged. In fact, the soft soil of the area was surprisingly undisturbed.

'Known round here as Bonkers' Copse, that is,' Larkin said. 'Mostly used by teenagers and the odd pros,' he added significantly, 'whose punter might like to do it Adam and Eve style. The scent of soil and grass and all that. But if she lived locally, the woman could have been taking a short cut. Like all parks, visitors mostly stick to the pathways but locals cut corners, don't they.'

Andy Lukeson's eyes followed the new path that wound snakelike away before turning back on itself to arrive back at a gate almost directly in line with the crime scene, and he appreciated PC Phil Larkin's reasoning. To follow the path would have taken the woman deeper into the park and the dark, losing what little benefit there was to be gained from the public lighting cast from the road (most of the lights in the park had been vandalized), and would have added to her journey.

Larkin looked beyond Lukeson to where Mel Burnett was in the company of a WPC. 'The child found the body. Must have been a shocker for the mite.'

Lukeson turned.

'Mother?' he asked, on seeing the woman holding the little girl by the hand.

'Yeah,' Larkin confirmed. 'Name's Burnett. Mel. Kid's name is Lucy, sir.'

Sir?

Only a couple of weeks before he and Larkin had shared a pint at the Plodder's Well (officially the King's Head, but nicknamed because of the stream of off duty and some on duty coppers from Loston nick who frequented the pub), confirmation of the gulf opening up by virtue of his rank, temporary though it might be.

Andy Lukeson was of a mind to tell Larkin, whom he had known since he had been a rookie under his wing five years previously, that he had not changed overnight and that Andy or Sarge would do fine. However, conscious of the age-old system of which, over time, he had become a part of as everyone did by intent or seduction (Sally Speckle might prove to be the exception), he considered that any relaxing of the formality of rank might not, at best, be appreciated by other DIs and the more senior ranks, and at

45

worst might begin a rot that would affect discipline in an organization that did not, by its nature of immediate and unequivocal response to an order, lend itself to democracy.

Lukeson had not yet reached a decision as to his place in the order of things, and would, even if Jack Porter packed it in and he was offered the job, probably revert to his former rank, not being comfortable in the new club he had joined.

He had never been an ambitious man, and he had a tendency to be outspoken, a character trait that in most organizations, though paid lip-service to, was the kiss of death. He had always believed that some were destined to lead, while others were best suited to play Watson to someone else's Holmes, and until he decided on the role he was most comfortable with, it would be most unfair of him to become the initiator of change, and then drop out to leave it to someone else to restore the status quo and earn the ill-feeling that his or her task of restoration would heap on the next chosen. If truth be told, he enjoyed being Sally Speckle's sergeant. She was a good guv'nor. But for how long, was the question. He had little doubt that if Speckle wanted to reach for the stars, there would be many willing hands to help her up.

Whereas he might end up like the tailend of a space shot that burns out and falls away as the rocket heads for the dizzy heights of outer space. But, of course, Porter's vacancy, should it arise, would likely be his last chance to break out of the ranks of detective sergeant.

'Best have a word then,' he said, going to speak to Mel and Lucy Burnett.

★   ★   ★

'Anything to contribute, Inspector?'

Caught on the hop, her thoughts elsewhere, DI Sally Speckle looked vaguely at ACC Mulgrave, trying desperately to cast her mind back to what had been said. Frank 'Sermon' Doyle's expression urged her to say something before she became the class idiot. 'Sorry,' did not suffice. Sensing DI Alldyce's smugness, Speckle was of a mind to wipe the grin off his face with the back of her hand. 'Slept badly, ma'am,' she said limply, and apologized again.

Mulgrave gave no indication that she accepted or rejected her explanation and apology. 'I've prepared a list of changes which I would like to see implemented.' Mulgrave proffered a file to Speckle. 'There's one for everyone. If you'll all read through it and let

47

me have your opinions, thoughts and suggestions within seven days.' The ACC stood up to leave. 'Must hurry along. Thank you all for your attendance and . . . ' she glanced at Speckle, and intoned, 'Interest.'

All present sprang to their feet and drifted out after Mulgrave.

'Speckle!' Sally came up short on Doyle's summons, her hope of escaping in the crowd up in smoke. 'A word.'

'You're in the shit now, girlie,' Alldyce murmured in an aside as he went past.

A colleague with him, added, 'Nothing in Uni has prepared you for a Doyle tongue-lashing, I dare say.'

'Tossers!'

'Close the door,' Doyle instructed. He gave her the full benefit of a satanic frown. 'What the devil were you playing at just now?' he demanded to know. 'Of all those present, you were the great white hope. Instead, you cocked up good and proper, didn't you. Slept badly my bum!'

Unquestionably at fault, there was no defence she could put forward (she could hardly offer as an excuse the fact that her head had been full of Simon Ambrose), so she endured Doyle's fiery rebuke and welcomed his more placatory plea: 'Sally, you've got a great career as a copper ahead of you. Don't toss it away by going absent when top brass are expecting you to give a lead. Mulgrave thinks that you're one of Loston's finest. Therein lies the opening of doors.'

'Yes, sir,' she said meekly, closing the door behind her, wondering seriously if Simon Ambrose walking back into her life had made the kind of earth-shattering difference that might sweep her future off in an entirely different direction?

4

'Mrs Burnett?'

The blonde-haired woman swung around. 'Not married. Don't believe in it. A lot of old twaddle, ain't it. Seen me mum and dad livin' in misery. I've a partner. Much better, that. Any time you want, you can pack a shopping bag and leg it.'

Andy Lukeson would not have agreed. His mum and dad lived blissfully in each other's pockets. 'I see,' he said, in the time-honoured police fashion to gain time when a plod has put his foot in it. 'DI Lukeson.' He turned his attention to the child. 'You must have been very frightened, young lady, finding a body.'

'What do you think,' Mel Burnett said aggressively.

'Frightened?' Lucy said with bravado. 'Me? Never.'

'But very brave too,' Lukeson said, in an attempt to make up lost ground with the youngster. But she was having none of it.

'Was she topped?' she asked, with the uninhibited forthrightness of the very young.

'Lucy!' her mum rebuked her.

'That's what coppers say on telly, mum,'

Lucy said, with the world-weary expression which the knowledgeable young reserve for their out-of-touch elders.

'We'll have to wait and see, young lady,' Lukeson said.

'Don't know why. She's all purple, the colour of me mum's anorak. And her tongue is hangin' out like so.' Lucy Burnett graphically poked her tongue out the side of her mouth.

'Will this take much longer?' Mel Burnett asked.

'Shouldn't think so,' Lukeson said.

Mel Burnett shivered. 'It's been an age already. I've got things to do,' she said huffily. 'Can't hang 'bout all day.'

'Did you see anyone?' Lukeson enquired of both.

Mel Burnett answered: 'It's a park. There's always people 'bout.'

'Anyone taking an interest in where the dead woman was found, maybe?'

'I was reading a mag.'

'Perhaps Lucy noticed someone?'

'Leave her out of this,' Mel Burnett pleaded. 'She's a six-year-old kid, for God's sake.'

'There was no one,' Lucy said positively.

'Thank you, Lucy,' Lukeson said. 'Don't I wish every witness was as good as you are.'

'Is that it?' Burnett pressed.

'For the present.'

'What d'ya mean, for the present?' Mel Burnett challenged.

'We'll need a statement, Ms Burnett. And we may need to speak with you again.'

'I've told you all I know.'

'And we appreciate your cooperation,' Andy Lukeson said smoothly. 'PC Larkin will drive you home now and take a brief statement.'

'If you ever find another body, keep your trap shut,' she scolded Lucy. 'Nothin' but trouble on your house, ain't it.'

Ignoring the rebuke, Lucy enquired excitedly of Phil Larkin, 'Will you put on your siren?'

'Not bloody likely,' Mel Burnett snapped. 'Don't want us arrivin' home with ev'ryone hangin' out the window.' She became thoughtful. 'I can't be sure, the way she looks now, but I think I've seen her 'round, the dead woman I mean.'

'Can you recall where you might have seen her?'

'Naw. Look, maybe I'm wrong. It's just that I have this feelin', ya know.'

'Please try to remember where you've seen her before, Ms Burnett,' Lukeson urged. 'It would be extremely helpful.'

The lines on Mel Burnett's forehead came together in concentration, but she shook her head. 'Can't think where. Sorry.'

'Well, if it comes back to you.'

'Yeah. Yeah. You reckon it was a punter who done for her?'

'A punter?'

'Yeah. She's a pros, right?'

'What makes you think that, Ms Burnett?'

Burnett shrugged. 'Don't rightly know. George Street ain't far away, is it.' George Street was Loston's redlight district. 'Ya know, maybe that's where I seen her. Used to work part time at the newsagent's on George Street. Might've come in for smokes, mightn't she.' Mel Burnett's face became suddenly bitter. 'If you ask me, the whole lot should be cleared off the streets.' Her dislike of prostitutes was obviously intense, and Andy Lukeson wondered why that was. Perhaps a partner who dabbled?

The dead woman had made no such impression on him. For one thing, her clothing wasn't right. Most prostitutes dressed to titillate: tight skirts and even tighter tops. But, of course, there were always the more quietly seductive kind, the upmarket escorts. But then what would an upmarket escort be doing in a grotty place like Bonkers' Copse? Plush hotels and limos were the order of the day in that league.

'Like coming to the park?' Lukeson innocuously enquired of Lucy Burnett, but with purpose.

Lucy hunched her small shoulders in a *take it or leave it* gesture.

'We get out as much as we can, don't we.' Mel Burnett ruffled the child's fair hair, hinting at an inner gentleness far removed from her outwardly brash personality. Lukeson wondered which persona was the predominant one in Mel Burnett. 'A shoebox has more room than the flat we live in.'

'Must be a bit cramped with three of you in it,' Lukeson said.

'Oh, mostly two. Robbo's away a lot.'

'Your partner?'

'Yeah. Robbo Crabby. He's a long-haul trucker. Around mostly at the weekends, except when he's on the sick. Likes his sickies, does Robbo. On one right now. Standard old pain in the back routine. Moanin' all day long 'til it's time to go to the boozer, then he's as fit as an Olympic sprinter. Lazy sod!'

It was obvious that Robbo Crabby was not the love of Mel Burnett's life.

'I bet you look just like your dad?' Lukeson said, playfully twigging Lucy's pert nose.

'No she ain't,' Mel denied quickly.

Andy Lukeson reckoned that Lucy was not

like Robbo Crabby, because he was not the child's father, which led him to believe that the only reason Mel Burnett was with Crabby was to provide a home of sorts for the little girl and herself until something or someone better happened along. Her next, unsolicited, statement confirmed the accuracy of his speculation.

'Can be a bad-tempered sod, Robbo. I mean, wouldn't you be, with a name like Crabby. Robbo Crabby. No great mystery I never tied the knot, is it. Who'd want to be called Mel Crabby, for God's sake.'

'I like going to the gym better,' Lucy said. 'It's warm there. Nice and clean, too. The park is yukky.' She giggled. 'Mum's got these great big muscles, ain't ya, mum?'

'I like to work out,' Mel Burnett told Lukeson. 'Great for gettin' rid of tension and frustration, workin' out.'

The loose-fitting anorak which she was wearing obviously hid the benefits of the gym as described by Lucy, although there was evidence in her strong neck muscles. The child's information began a train of thought for Lukeson — *great big muscles* echoed in his mind, the kind of muscles that would give Mel Burnett the strength to kill, perhaps?

But why would Mel Burnett want to murder the woman?

It was wild speculation, of course. However, in his experience, wild speculation often proved close to the mark. Burnett had vehemently enunciated her dislike of prostitutes, a prejudice born of something which had happened? Might the bold Robbo like to fool around? Though Mel Burnett was not an educated woman, Lukeson suspected that she did not lack intelligence. So if she was in any way involved in the death of the woman, why would she raise the idea that she had seen her before and specifically launch the notion that she had been a prostitute? Might it be that by so doing she would hope to deflect attention from herself? Was Mel Burnett that devious a person? Was she also ruthless enough to have her child find the body she had left to be found? Which would in essence make *her* the finder.

So what might her motive be? If every woman murdered the prostitute her husband or partner was involved with, it would solve in spit-quick time the problem of prostitution Revenge, of course, was an age-old motive for murder. However, if as it appeared, Robbo Crabby was simply a convenience for Mel Burnett until something better happened along, why would she get so worked up about anything he got up to?

Unless . . .

A dark thought crept out of Andy Lukeson's subconscious, What if the dead woman was a favourite of Robbo Crabby's? And what if he had brought home to Mel a very unwelcome visitor by his association with her?

Anger was also a very common motive for murder.

'Live close by, do you, Ms Burnett?' he enquired conversationally.

'Vine street. Only a street away. Makes the park convenient to come to.'

On the doorstep of the crime scene, too. A sudden yawning hole appeared in Andy Lukeson's speculation. How would Mel Burnett have known that the murdered woman would be in the park?

'Must be hard rearing a kid on your own, except when your partner's at home to share the burden,' Lukeson said.

'At home,' she scoffed. 'Then Robbo's usually down the pub, if he's got the readies.'

'Has he a favourite?'

'Pub, you mean?'

'Yes. Most men do, don't they.'

'Robbo ain't choosy. But he don't travel far, 'cause it's difficult to get home with legs that are sloshin' beer, know what I mean? Usually found in the Coachman's Inn.' Lukeson knew of the pub: a haunt of society's less desirables, the kind of place one might frequent if one were looking for the illicit or the illegal. 'Let's be gettin' you home, then.' She took Lucy's hand and squeezed it companionably. Whatever Mel Burnett's faults were, it was obvious she dearly loved her daughter.

'My ball, mum!'

'I'll get ya 'nother ball.'

'But I want — '

'I said I'll get ya 'nother ball!'

'Where is your ball, Lucy?' Lukeson asked. 'I'm a policeman. Maybe I can find it for you.'

'I know where it is. It's in them bushes where the woman is.'

'How did it get in there?'

'Mum threw it and it went in there. That's how I found her.'

'Oh, dear,' Lukeson said. 'It'll have to stay there I'm afraid, Lucy. You see, the bushes are what we now call a crime scene, and nothing can be removed from there until the police have examined it. Understand?'

'Of course I understand,' Lucy Burnett said, as if she were dealing with an idiot. 'You've got to wait until the SOCOs are finished.'

'You watch too much bloody telly,' Mel Burnett scolded her daughter, dragging Lucy with her.

58

'Before you go. You said that you thought you knew the woman. Did you enter the crime scene?'

'Glanced in through the bushes.'

'But you didn't actually enter it?' Lukeson checked.

'That would be a daft thing to do.'

'Yes, it would,' Lukeson agreed.

Why daft? Daft because of her natural revulsion? Or daft because had she visited the scene of crime traces of her might be found there? Why should she want to avoid that happening, if she were innocent? Would a perfectly innocent person even think of that? On the other hand, if she had murdered the dead woman, might there not be traces of her there already? And by revisiting the scene a reason why such traces were found would have been established, which could only be of help to her were she the killer. Did all of that point to guilt or innocence? Or just a policeman clutching at straws?

'And you, young lady. Did you touch anything?' Lukeson enquired.

'Touch anything?' she said, her face curling in disgust. 'Gross.'

'Why do you ask?' Mel Burnett enquired.

'Just trying to get a complete picture to help us with our enquiries,' Lukeson said.

'I didn't reckon we were part of your

59

enquiries to start with, Inspector,' Mel Burnett said tersely.

'Oh, it's just procedure,' Lukeson said off handedly. 'A copper's life is one long procedure.'

Andy Lukeson looked after Mel Burnett, frowning thoughtfully. Had she thrown the ball into the bushes for Lucy to fetch? For her to find the body? Might his speculation not be that wild after all? What if Robbo Crabby had gone to the Coachman's Inn? And what if Mel Burnett, possibly suspecting something, had followed him? Saw him with the woman and, enraged, followed her when she left the pub?

Mel Burnett was a very fit and strong woman. The murdered woman seemed to be in good shape, but in a female rather than a muscular way. Burnett was smaller than the victim, which would be to her disadvantage, but her muscularity would probably cancel out the victim's height advantage. Was his a likely theory? Or wishful thinking? Was he, in his anxiety to do well on his first solo murder investigation, in fact grasping at any wildcat theory rather than having none at all?

He had only arrived on scene ten minutes ago, but he could not shake the feeling that he should be further along. Lord, fifteen years a copper and experiencing first-time nerves.

Now he fully understood Sally Speckle's edginess at the beginning of an investigation. Like him, it was no doubt down to the fear with each new case that the investigation would grind to an inglorious dead end and become that dreaded spectre of a police officer's existence — a cold case.

5

'Good morning, Andy.' The police surgeon's cheery greeting cut in on Lukeson's thoughts. Alec Balson ducked under the tape cordoning off the crime scene. 'Let you out on your own, eh,' he said mischievously. 'Heard you took over from Porter.'

'And right now I'm not at all sure that I did myself any favours,' Lukeson said sourly.

'Missing her nibs holding your hand, are you?' Lukeson glared at Balson. 'Ooops! Touched a raw nerve, have I?' He went ahead of Lukeson, looking about at the debris-strewn scene of crime. 'Not a nice place to end up in, is it. And,' looking about him, 'with all this muck about, it will be a forensics nightmare.' Striding ahead, he added with pragmatic detachment, his senses blunted over the years by constant contact with sickness and death, 'Done for, you know. Porter, I mean.' Lukeson knew Alec Balson to be a kindly and caring man and doctor, but like many in his profession he had had to learn not to become burdened with the downside of his profession. 'A bang as big as he had does a lot of damage. I doubt very much at his age, with a couple of years to go, if he'll think it worth the bother, and more so the risk. Not a relaxed person, Jack Porter.'

'That's not the opinion at the nick. Word is that he can't wait to get back in the saddle.'

'It might be his wish, but I doubt if it'll become fact, Andy. Being a bachelor took its toll. Not taking proper care. Too many late nights in the Plodders Well. Junk food . . . '

'A policeman's lot. It's a bloody miracle that so many officers manage to reach pension age to begin with.'

'That's why fellows like you need a wife, Andy. Nothing like a wife to see to your fats and sugars.' He grinned. 'That is, of course, unless she suspects a younger model is hidden away for fun and games.' His grin widened. 'Or the shoe is on the other foot, and the missus has a whacking great insurance policy on you, the proceeds of which she wants to spend with a young stud.'

'You're in a cheery mood, I must say,' Lukeson said, deadpan.

Balson knelt beside the body, and adjusted the steel-framed spectacles he wore which Sally Speckle had mentioned made him look sinister under the right light. Lukeson had thought her impression fanciful, but now in the intensely lit murder scene, the light made all the brighter by the darkness of the day and the concentration of light due to the over-grown bushes, he could see why she might think Balson looked sinister. 'Strangled. Not manual.' He examined the dead woman's neck closely then, thoughtfully, he took the light scarf he was wearing and wound it in a tight band. He lifted the woman's head and slipped the scarf round her neck, and then compared the bruised circles on her neck, and murmured, 'Heavier. Possibly woollen. If we're lucky . . . ' He examined the woman's hands individually, leaning close to scrutinize the nails. 'Nothing, I'm afraid,' was his deflated conclusion. 'But it looks like she's got an earring missing.' He turned the dead woman's head to show her left ear, which had no earring compared to her right ear which had a discreet clip-on earring which, for Lukeson, was another pointer to the dead woman not being a prostitute. Perhaps he was being a little critical (he preferred that to snobbish), but for him a prostitute would have worn earrings that were more brash. Probably great brass loops. Or was that a caricature?

'Sandra Fairweather,' Lukeson murmured thoughtfully.

'Sandra Fairweather?' Balson queried.

'Three years ago, Sandra Fairweather was found murdered in Cobley Wood.'

'The same wood that figured prominently

in Sally Speckle's first case, as I recall.'[1]

'Yes, it was,' Lukeson confirmed. 'Fairweather was found at the northern end of the wood, which made it Brigham's problem, thankfully, because it remains unsolved.'

'Oh, yes.' He looked with concern at Andy Lukeson. 'Strangled, also.'

'Yes.'

'And you're thinking, same killer?'

'The thought came to mind,' Lukeson said.

'Three years ago. A very patient killer, if he's only killed again now,' Balson said.

'Maybe he doesn't get the killing urge very often,' Lukeson said. 'Or he could have been banged up for something else, and has only recently been let out? Or,' Andy Lukeson's face became a mask of dark worry, 'maybe we just haven't found the killer's other victims?'

'Similarities between this woman and Fairweather?' Balson queried.

'None really, except maybe ages. Fairweather was younger, but not by much. Dark haired, this victim is blonde. Brown eyes, blue this time. And Fairweather was smaller and heavier.'

'Probably just a coincidence, Andy.'

'Maybe,' Lukeson conceded. He frowned, his sigh weary. 'Thing is, I'm not really a

_____
[1] See *Pick Up*.

65

believer in coincidence, Alec.'

'Well, it's a line of inquiry,' Balson said.

The police surgeon examined the dead woman more intently, and went through the routine of establishing the approximate time of death, concluding: 'Dead about ten hours.'

Lukeson checked his watch.

'Killed about midnight then?'

'Leeway of an hour either side.'

'So, somewhere between 11 p.m. and 1 a.m.'

'To be going on with. The post-mortem will tighten up the time. And it looks like the intention was murder, plain and simple. No sign of sexual activity evident. Forensic Pathology might differ, but I don't expect so.'

Lukeson's interest was caught by the earth close to the body, and the clear path leading away from it, like earth which had been recently raked over. His eyes followed the line of the path into the bushes to the rear of the crime scene, his gaze coming to rest on a discarded leafy branch of a sapling, tell-tale earth clinging to it.

Alec Balson gave voice to the detective's thoughts. 'Clever fellow, Andy. Swept the ground to obliterate his footprints as he left. A cool, well-organized customer like that won't be easy to nab.'

Lukeson agreed. The killer's action showed

meticulousness and calmness, maybe planning also. Which would put to rest his first thoughts that the woman's murder might have been opportunistic. A great part of getting away with murder was good planning, meticulous attention to detail, a calm and cool head, and all those elements were evident in the killer's careful retreat from the murder scene. But why had the killer gone to the bother of leaving through the thick bushes to the rear of the crime scene when he could have left by the more accessible front entrance to Bonkers' Copse? Would he or she not have wanted to be away as quickly as possible? The reason had to lie at the other side of the thick undergrowth to the rear of the scene. Lukeson went to check, and the reason became instantly clear. The stony underlay for a new path which had not yet been laid would rule out any hope of a footprint, and a vandalized overhead light would have meant total darkness, because a row of trees cut off light from the nearby road. Had the killer left the other way he or she would have risked being seen. A person sweeping the ground with the branch of a sapling would stick in the mind, and a functioning overhead light would make the murderer perfectly visible and therefore describable, and there was a dry concrete path (rain had not fallen for most of a week, but the scene of crime, dank as it was, was damp), which would offer a perfect canvass for muddy footprints.

Conclusion: either the killer came prepared, or was a very cool customer indeed, obliterating his or her footprints as he or she left. The trainers Mel Burnett had been wearing came to mind. Trainers would leave a very traceable patterned footprint. However, the killer's cleverness might work against him or her, because making a path through the thick bushes would be forensically risky, and might offer up vital trace evidence. Swings and roundabouts, Lukeson thought. Swings and roundabouts. With Burnett in mind, he enquired of Balson, 'Could the killer be a woman, Alec?'

'Possible,' he murmured, obviously not too taken with the idea. 'The dead woman would be no pushover. Fit. Good muscle tone. So if her killer was a woman, even with surprise on her side, she'd have to be pretty strong and agile.'

'Someone who'd keep fit. Work out regularly.'

'And probably pop the odd illegal steroid, too, I shouldn't wonder.'

Lukeson thought that the odd illegal steroid might not prove too difficult to get hold of where Mel Burnett lived. And there was something else: the trainers Mel Burnett had been wearing when he spoke to her were spotless — in fact, blemish free and spanking new. Coincidence? Or had she been wearing new trainers because she'd dumped the pair she'd worn for murder?

SOCO were waiting in the wings for Balson to finish, and the body, prepared by Balson for removal, was taken away before beginning their examination of the detritus-strewn crime scene which Andy Lukeson looked around despondently.

'A bit of a tip, isn't it,' the SOCO team leader groaned, and added glumly, looking about at the accumulated filth, 'It'll take an age to sift through; to sort out what's relative and what's incidental. A great deal of it will have been windblown and trapped, and just totally innocent rubbish. But the job will be to determine what's relevant to the murder and murderer, and what's not.'

Before letting the SOCOs get on with it, Andy Lukeson explained to the team leader his ideas on how the killer had left the scene, the relevance of the bushes through which he or she had had to squeeze, and their possible value as a source of trace evidence.

'I'd have never guessed,' was his narky reply, obviously resenting, as he saw it, being told how to do his job, unjustifiably so in Lukeson's opinion, he being the officer tasked with catching the murderer. However, though piqued, he could understand the SOCO officer's reaction. No man, particularly one with a detailed and expert knowledge of his job, like Jack Hanley had, liked to be, as he would see it, talked down to.

'Jack Hanley often suffers from tight underpants syndrome,' Balson said, as he and Lukeson took their leave. 'Particularly when he has those dark circles under his eyes after a bender. Right now, I'd say every rustle of every leaf sends shafts of pain through his head.'

Lukeson said, 'But even half-pissed, he's the best in the business. No sign of sexual activity, you say, Alec?'

'Nothing obvious.'

'Then you don't think she was on the game?'

'Oh, I see. Redlight district to hand.'

'It's a thought, isn't it?'

'Doesn't strike me as a prostitute, Andy. She was murdered around midnight,' Balson pointed out. 'If she was a prostitute there would surely be irrefutable evidence of sexual activity.'

'Maybe she started work late, Alec? Maybe her killer was her first punter of the night?'

'A lot of maybes, Andy.'

'There always are. All you've got at the early stage of a murder investigation are ifs and maybes, until the fog begins to lift.'

'And you think, or rather fear, that this time it won't?' Alec Balson was a shrewd, astute, and a very perceptive man. 'The killer might never have had sex on his mind to begin with.'

'Murder from the off?'

Balson shrugged. 'Another if, another maybe, Andy. But if it was sex, then the punter was way down market. Nowadays, even at the human hamburger end of the chain, a car would be a minimum require-ment. The days of up against the alley wall or a place like this are gone.'

'Unless by specific request,' Lukeson said. 'The killer might have liked the grotty surroundings as a turn-on?'

Balson's mobile rang. 'Yes, Shirley. I'll be there shortly. Got to go. Surgery filling up.'

'Give me your report as soon as you can.'

Balson nodded in the direction of the murder scene. 'Good luck. You'll need a rub of the green on this one, Andy.' His reminder, Luke-son thought, he might have kept to himself.

Might the murder scene be a place where Robbo Crabby, drunk, on foot, would bring a woman? And what if he was a regular, and

Mel Burnett knew about his place of preference? The problem was, if Crabby was with the murdered woman, how would Mel Burnett kill the woman? With the mental picture of Crabby, given by Mel, chivalry would not be his strong point, so was it not possible that satisfied, he'd up and leave and not bother seeing her back to her patch, letting a gap in time into which Mel could have stepped to commit murder.

Of course, there was one other possibility, and that was that Crabby had done for her.

Andy Lukeson looked to the busy road beyond the park and the row of old Victorian houses, spacious rooms divided by stud walls to convert them to as many flats per house as was humanly possible to maximize the landlord's return. If she had taken a short cut through the park, the dead woman might very well have lived in one of the houses.

'Jack . . . '

'Yeah,' Hanley answered, his manner abrupt, his concentration on the crime scene now total and not welcoming of interruption.

'What impression does the dead woman make on you?'

'Impression?'

'What would you guess her occupation to have been?'

'Office type. Could be a professional woman.'

'Professional?'

Jack Hanley chuckled. 'Not that kind of profession, Andy. Someone on the game becomes hard; they get a *look*. She doesn't have that. No ID, then?'

'No.'

'Can't have been theft anyway. Her handbag was left behind, with almost forty quid in it.'

'But the killer must have taken her ID. She'd surely have had to have something that would indentify her in her bag.

'Maybe her ID linked her to her killer? Hubby. Boyfriend.' He studied Lukeson. 'How do you like being cut loose from Speckle, then?'

'Only out on loan, I reckon, Jack.'

'You sound like you didn't want to be cut loose, Andy.'

Lukeson thought that Hanley may have hit the nail on the head.

'Poor bitch.' Lukeson spun round on DC Helen Rochester. 'What a place to have it all end.'

'What're you doing here?' he groused.

'Thanks a lot,' Rochester said, but in an easy manner that showed she had not taken offence. 'For my sins, which must be black and many, I'm to be your acting DS.'

'You?'

'Don't make it sound like you've found something nasty on the sole of your shoe, Andy.'

'That'll be — ' Lukeson bit his tongue.

'Sir?' Rochester intoned coolly. 'Fine with me.'

'Oh, don't take any notice. I'm being an arsehole, Helen.'

'Some things never change.'

Lukeson looked at her severely, before they both burst in to laughter. 'Did your guv'nor have a hand in this? Maybe Sally Speckle thought that I wasn't ready to be let out on my own, eh?'

'She had nothing to do with it.'

'Did she tell you that?'

'No, she didn't.'

'Then how can you be so bloody sure?' Lukeson charged.

'Because she was dead against. Me being seconded was Doyle's idea. You needed a DS, so here I am. But if you don't — '

'Oh, shut up. Between you and me, I'm pretty pleased that you were seconded, Helen.'

'Flattery,' she chirped, and rubbed a hand across her brow like a Victorian maiden who had been snatched from the shelf by the handsome hero. 'Whatever next, Mr Lukeson. Why, I'm all a titter, sir.'

'Very droll.'

'Doyle said that Ron Scott, Porter's DS, and you would be petrol to flame. It's fairly quiet, so here I am.'

On one hand, Lukeson was pleased that Rochester would be working with him, because Doyle had got it right about him and Scott. However, on the other hand, he wasn't at all sure that he shouldn't challenge the decision and give Scott no quarter. Stamp his authority, so to speak. Because if he was offered Porter's vacancy, should it arise, Scott would be his permanent DS. So it might be better to brook no nonsense right from the word go. However, were he to make an issue of it, it would put Rochester in a tight spot through no fault of her own, and there was no guarantee that Doyle would be for turning. The Chief Super was a man who tended to stick with a decision, once made.

DS Scott and he had history of long standing, stretching back over years, a history Lukeson wasn't at all sure he understood, because as rookies he and Scott had got on reasonably well. Having Rochester seconded was not the best start, and Scott would brag about having given his new Acting DI the finger.

Sensing Lukeson's unease, Helen Rochester said, 'You're not over the moon about this, are you, Andy? Look, if you want, you can get on your high horse, boot me out, and make Scott tow the line. It wouldn't do the prat any harm to be brought down a peg or two.'

'Doyle wouldn't wear it.'

'And if he did?'

'Our CS is a stubborn man who doesn't like his decisions questioned, Helen.'

'That's not a good enough reason to let yourself be walked on, Andy.'

'Walked on? That's a bit strong.'

'I'll phone my guv'nor and — '

'And do what?' Lukeson barked. 'I'm bloody glad you're here, Helen.'

'That's good to know, Andy. But I'll understand if you feel a right twit and come out of your corner fighting.'

'Thanks. But Doyle is right. Scott and I would be at each other's throats in no time at all.'

'Don't you have any ambition, Lukeson?' the Chief Super had questioned when he had been offered Porter's vacancy, obviously befuddled by meeting a man who had not. 'Stepping into Porter's shoes is a slap on the back, personally delivered by Alice Mulgrave, incidentally.'

Lukeson had been surprised that the decision to promote him had not been Doyle's. He had naturally assumed that it had been.

'She thinks you've got potential.'

'And you, sir?'

'Goes without saying.' Doyle had groaned much the same as a teacher with a particularly recalcitrant child might. 'Don't get shitty about this, Lukeson.'

Lukeson had not at all been sure that Doyle was being honest and not diplomatic, and he could not resist putting that to him. Doyle took no time at all to answer.

'You've rumbled me, Andy. No, you wouldn't have been my first choice.'

'Thank you for your candour, sir, if belated.'

'Don't get shirty! I think Scott should have got a shot at stepping into his guv'nor's shoes. It's not because Scott is a better copper. He's no Sherlock bloody Holmes, but he's a good honest copper who's worked hard on curbing Porter's, shall we say, exuberance. Porter got results, but not always by the book. Had Scott not pulled his leash now and then all sorts of nasties would have hit the fan. So by my reckoning, that diligence should have been rewarded. Scott was heir to the throne, you might say. But Mulgrave doesn't believe in that sort of thing.'

'A strange one, Scott,' Lukeson said. 'Content to play second fiddle to Porter all these years, when everyone knew that it was Scott who often steered Porter on to the right track. But he never took the credit. Seemed happy enough to let Porter bask in the glory, while he slunk away to the shadows.'

Doyle studied Lukeson.

'You don't know, do you?'

'Know? Know what?'

'About Scott and Porter. What bloody planet have you been on, Lukeson?'

Like a flash out of the blue, Andy Lukeson understood.

'Never interfered with their work,' Doyle said. 'So I never let on. In fact, no one round here did.' Doyle shook his head. 'The gruff Porter and the wrestler like Scott. But there you have it. Takes all sorts.'

Now, after four years of bad blood between him and Scott, Andy Lukeson understood. His mind went back to a short period during which Porter had moved in with him while his house was being renovated after a kitchen fire. It was soon afterwards that Scott had reported him for a minor breach of regulations during the search of a suspect's house, which Scott had blown out of all proportion.

Jealousy.

After, when Porter had moved back home, Scott had made several attempts to mend fences but he wasn't having any of it.

'So, like to bring me up to speed, Andy?' Helen Rochester's question brought Lukeson back to the present. 'That is, if you're not sending me packing.'

Rochester listened intently to what facts were known, which were few and far between, and to Lukeson's speculation about how Mel Burnett might fit into the picture, and the motive she might have had for killing the dead woman. 'And, of course, Robbo Crabby has to be kept in mind.'

'Mel Burnett,' Rochester intoned. 'Might it be that you're opting for the old hoary idea of the discoverer of the body, which in essence she was, being the first suspect, Andy,' she stated with her usual bluntness.

'There's been a few over time,' he pointed out. 'And Mel Burnett did throw the ball into the bushes.'

'You can't be sure of that,' Rochester stated. 'A thrown ball can go anywhere, can't it? Mel Burnett would have to be some cold-blooded bitch to do that to her own kid, Andy.'

Thinking back on how fond Mel Burnett had seemed to be of Lucy, Lukeson had to agree.

Obviously Rochester thought the idea to be off the wall, and she may very well be right. However, Lukeson had learned by experience that it was wise not to discard any notion, no matter how outrageous, particularly at the outset of an investigation, if only to get the investigative juices flowing. And of course, any theories were better than no theories at all. 'Police work is like science fiction, ain't it,' a wily old DC had told him as a rookie, when a most unlikely theory in a post office robbery became the outcome. 'Sometimes the fiction becomes, daft as it seems at the time, fact, lad.' It was a comparison that had served him well in countless investigations. 'Might be a load of old cobblers.' the DC had said. 'But then it might not be, too.'

Some killers, usually those who were not natural killers, could not stand the anxiety of the period between murder and discovery and were sometimes driven to bring their deed out in the open to relieve that anxiety.

Lukeson checked his watch.

'Eleven fifteen. A coffee wouldn't go astray right now. My treat.'

Helen Rochester sighed, and fluttered her eyelids.

'Oh, you spoil me, sir.'

Acting DI Andy Lukeson grinned. 'Give over!'

He was leaving when Hanley hailed him, holding up something with a tweezers. 'Snagged on a bush.' He pointed to the rear of the crime scene, the route which Lukeson reckoned the murderer had left by.

Lukeson went to see what Hanley had found. It was a yellow wool thread. From the murder weapon, possibly?

6

'Ma'am . . . '

DI Sally Speckle looked vaguely at DC Charlie Johnson. 'Sorry, Charlie. A bit preoccupied today.'

'We all get those kind of days,' Johnson said generously. 'Anyway, it's all pretty boring stuff at the moment.' Johnson had been running through the cases which were currently being investigated. 'A couple of car thefts. A GBH, which is more or less tied up. And as I was outlining just now, a burglary.'

'Oh, for a nice juicy murder,' WPC Anne Fenning sighed.

'It's nice to be slumming for a change,' was PC Brian Scuttle's opinion.

'Saw Ms Mulgrave arriving this morning,' Johnson said. 'Looking very determined, I must say.'

It was Johnson's way of asking about what had gone on at the meeting with Mulgrave in Doyle's office, but Speckle was not of a mind to discuss it. She'd much prefer to return to the quite elicit thoughts she had been having about Simon Ambrose.

'Any progress on the burglary, Charlie?' she

enquired, more to be seen to be interested rather than actually being interested.

'Might have been a ghost. Didn't leave a trace.'

'Who was burgled?'

'The Lamplins. Cecily Lamplin to be precise.'

'Lamplin? Rings a bell somewhere.'

'Of gardening fame,' Johnson said. 'Has a whole raft of gardening books to his credit. Would have made a great scrum half for England, they say, before polio struck him down on a visit to India when he was nineteen years old. Not a bad sort. The proceeds from his latest book *Gardening For The Physically Impaired* are going to the disabled. Apparently he still has problems himself sometimes, the lingering after-effects of polio act up now and then.'

'Done your homework, haven't you?' Speckle said.

'Not really, guv. Read it on the dust jacket of his latest book.'

'I didn't know you were in to gardening,' Brian Scuttle said. 'Thought you spent all your time chasing birds.' He grinned. 'In the hope that one would hang about long enough to be caught.'

'You're hilarious,' Johnson snorted. 'You should try a career in comedy. Keep you nice and slim, because you wouldn't earn enough to eat.'

'Oopps!' Scuttle taunted. 'Tweaked a raw nerve have I, Charlie?'

'Shut it!' said WPC Anne Fenning.

'You surprise me, Charlie,' Speckle said.

'I bet that's what all the girls say,' Scuttle sniggered.

'Shut it!' Fenning barked.

'Somehow, I couldn't see you forking out your hard-earned cash for a gardening book,' Speckle finished.

'I didn't. Library. Browsing. Lamplin has a great style,' Johnson enthused. 'You'd never believe how he can make something as dull sound so interesting. Weaves history into the text. Things like the flowers and plants Adolf Hitler liked. Or Napoleon. And it seems Julius Caesar suffered chronic hay fever.'

'Should anyone care?' Scuttle groaned.

'These kind of details fascinate some people, Brian,' Speckle said. 'I mean if you were a Nazi, wouldn't you want Hitler's favourite flowers in your garden.

'To each his own madness, I say,' WPC Anne Fenning said.

'Much taken in the burglary?' Speckle enquired of Johnson.

'Jewellery.'

'Valuable?'

'An antique diamond tiara and necklace that was a Lamplin family heirloom. Dug this up.' Johnson produced a glossy magazine photograph of Cecily Lamplin, Lamplin's wife, wearing the jewellery at a musical evening for a Loston charity. 'What our American friends would call a thousand dollars a plate bash.'

'Insured, I take it?'

'A hundred thousand, guv. And before you get on to the wrong track, a hundred thousand would be small change to the Lamplins.'

'Any sign of the jewellery being off-loaded?'

Charlie Johnson shook his head. 'A check on all the usual suspects hasn't thrown anything up. But I never expected that it would. This stuff won't see the light of day until well after the dust has settled.'

'Usual suspects?'

'Three with a fondness for all that glitters. Ian Formby, Jack Glass and Hannah Frampton. The first two are inside — '

'And Frampton?'

'At her apartment in Monaco.'

'Monaco?'

'Yeah.'

'Which gives the lie to the idea that crime doesn't pay, eh,' Brian Scuttle grumbled.

'You'll not see an apartment in Monaco on a copper's pension, for certain.'

'Checked out, of course?' Speckle asked Johnson.

'Police and her doctor. She's in bed with flu presently.'

'An out-of-towner, then?' Anne Fenning speculated.

He shrugged. 'Checking on anyone who might have paid Loston a visit in the days prior to the robbery.'

'Prints?'

Johnson shook his head.

'Anything?'

'Like I said, might as well have been a ghost, guv.'

'Word on the street, then?'

'Brass monkey syndrome. Me sees nothing. Me hears nothing. Me says nothing.'

'No one can break into a place, nick valuable and readily identifiable jewellery and vanish into thin air, Charlie,' Speckle said.

'A tall order indeed,' Johnson agreed. 'But, as of now, that seems to have been what happened.'

'Making a din, is he'?' PC Brian Scuttle asked. 'A well-connected bloke like Lamplin.'

'Not a tittle.'

'Strange. Wouldn't you say, ma'am?'

'Lamplin might be the kind who leaves

matters to the police, Brian.'

'And I'm the Pope,' Scuttle snorted. 'Blokes like him always know someone they can put the screw on. And they're never slow to do so.'

'So what do you think happened, Charlie?' Speckle enquired of the DC.

'My report is on computer, guv.'

'Yes. But computers, though very efficient at recording facts, are hopeless when it comes to getting across thoughts and feelings and hunches. The policeman's famous gut instinct.'

DC Charlie Johnson thought for a spell before answering cautiously, 'I'm not sure that I buy the story, ma'am.'

'Based on what?'

'Cecily Lamplin was in the house when the robbery took place. She saw a stray dog rummaging in a newly planted flower bed. Went outside, leaving the patio doors open. She'd only be a couple of minutes . . . '

'Patio doors. To the front or the rear of the house, Charlie?'

'Rear.'

'Close to the road?'

'No.'

'How far from the road then?'

'The house is at the end of a long drive, standing with about equal distance from the road to the front and another equally impressive house to the rear.'

'That pretty much rules out a passing thief spotting an opportunity, doesn't it,' Speckle said thoughtfully. 'The open patio doors was the route in, presumably?'

'That's the theory, guv.'

'Wouldn't the burglar have been spotted by Mrs Lamplin?' Fenning said, 'if she was in the garden.'

'When I said garden, I didn't mean a patch of grass,' Johnson said. 'You could play war games in it. Full of nooks and crannies. The flowerbed Cecily Lamplin was working on is well away from the house in a shaded nook, surrounded by trees and bushes. She wouldn't have had a clear sight of the house. And consequently, the burglar would not have had clear sight of her.'

'Dogs?' Speckle asked.

'The Lamplins don't like dogs. Too fond of rooting up things. And the Lamplin gardens are a good match for Versailles. And therefore not canine friendly.'

'Private sorts, the Lamplins?' Speckle asked.

'Yes, guv. Rupert Lamplin's got a website, but there's nothing personal on it. Mostly about Lamplin's horticulture expertise and his books. Doesn't court publicity or seek attention, it would seem. The odd charity bash. Likes opera. Which was where they were going on the day the burglary took place. That was the reason Cecily Lamplin had her best gear laid out on the bed.'

'What time did the burglary take place?'

'Cecily Lamplin reported the theft at 3.16 p.m.'

'So why would she lay out the clothes she would wear to the opera that night so early?' Speckle pondered.

'If I'm going clubbing I would, guv,' Fenning said. 'Actually, I'd spend the afternoon mixing and matching.'

'You should rely more on your natural beauty,' Scuttle said tongue-in-cheek.

'Get stuffed, Brian,' Fenning responded.

'OK,' Speckle said. 'Assuming that the Lamplins' aversion to dogs is not well known, one would expect that such a house would have canines wandering about. It would be par for the course with people like the Lamplins. So put yourself in the burglar's shoes. A long drive with lots of bushes and shrubbery from where a surly pit bull dog could launch an attack. Approaching from the rear, there would be that other house to worry about. Someone glancing out a window and the game would be up. Add in extraordinary eyesight to be able to spot those open patio doors from a long way off . . . '

'Binoculars, guv,' Scuttle said.

'That would suggest that the house was being watched,' Johnson said. 'And with trees to the front and rear of the Lamplin house, getting a clear view of the house could be a problem for a prospective thief?'

'And CCTV?' Speckle continued.

'No CCTV,' Johnson said.

'No CCTV,' Speckle, Fenning and Scuttle chorused incredulously.

'Cecily Lamplin has this thing about being watched,' Johnson explained.

'I'm getting a picture here of a very odd couple, and a very odd set-up, Charlie,' Speckle said.

'I hate cameras. I hate being watched. You can't turn now without someone watching you,' Charlie Johnson complained. 'CCTV has become all-pervasive.'

'CCTV prevents crime,' Fenning argued.

'I'm not convinced that it does,' Brian Scuttle said.

'Burgo alarm?'

'Immobilized, guv. The lady of the house was at home.'

'Shut it!' Speckle ordered, as the argument between Fenning and Scuttle about the benefits or non-benefits of CCTV continued on the wings, becoming more and more animated. 'Another thing, even if a cheeky chappie did risk it, someone could have been inside the house. Waiting to pounce on the thief when he entered. Gates?'

'Electronically controlled,' Johnson informed.

'As is the norm in that neck of the woods?'

'Boundary walls?'

'High and thick enough to hold Genghis Khan at bay.'

Speckle's mobile rang.

'Lunch?' Simon Ambrose said, in the softly seductive way he could when at his most charming.

'Can't get away,' she replied, conscious of eyes on her.

'You're the boss. Of course you can. One o'clock be OK? I won't take no for an answer, Sally. You come to me, or I'll go round and fetch you.'

'What can I say.'

'Yes. Lorenzo's. One o'clock.' Speckle was taken aback. Lorenzo's was not a caf. 'A bit of luck on a nag,' he explained.

'I didn't know you gambled. You never did when we were — '

'A lot changes in ten years, Sally,' he interjected, his voice sadly reflective.

'It must have been a sizeable bit of luck.'

'It was,' Ambrose said, almost curtly, as if he did not like being questioned. His next remark confirmed this. 'Always the copper, eh. See you at one o'clock.' He broke the connection, cutting off her next excuse for not being able to comply with his wishes? Or perhaps to stymie any further debate about the changes which had taken place over the years? And she wondered how many changes might there have been. She realized, in fact, that Simon Ambrose was pretty much a stranger to her, as she must be to him.

When she returned her gaze to those present, eyes averted, she was going to say something about an old friend but changed her mind. There was no obligation on her to explain anything that was outside of their common interest as police officers, which she got back to immediately. 'Another chat with Cecily Lamplin might be in order, Charlie,' she said.

7

'Coffee?' enquired the barmaid, bewildered by a request that, to say the least, was seldom made in a pub like the Coachman's Inn.

'Two,' Andy Lukeson said. 'One white, and?' He looked to Helen Rochester.

'Black. No sugar.'

'I'll do me best,' she said, and vanished through a door behind the bar, which gave a glimpse of a carpeted hallway lined either side with crates of beer.

'Get the feeling we're not very welcome?' Rochester said.

'As welcome as Satan in a church, I'd say.'

He turned and looked round at the sparsely occupied bar and those present, huddled as if they had formed a common defence against a common enemy. The Coachman's Inn was, in copper parlance, known to the police. It was a hangout for the junior ranks of Loston's criminal fraternity, pushers and prostitutes. It was where a great many plots were hatched, deals done, and many pick-ups made. Many of the women who plied their trade in the nearby redlight district of George Street dropped in.

There was one man, dark-hair, too dark for his age — a toupee — sitting at a table in an out-of-the-way nook near the loos, who was even more uneasy than the rest. He was clearly wishing that he was some other place, any place at all but where he found himself.

He looked out of place.

'Reckon if we fingerprinted this lot we'd have a lengthy print-out of form,' Rochester opined.

The door behind the bar opened and the barmaid came back bearing two mugs of coffee, which she slapped down on the bar. 'That's the best I can do,' she said, the subtext being: take it or leave, see if I care.

'Bikkies?' Lukeson enquired.

'You've got a sense of humour,' the barmaid snorted, 'I'll say that for ya. Bikkies,' she intoned and laughed. Lukeson placed his warrant card on the bar. 'Might have bloody known!'

'And DS Rochester,' Lukeson said, leaving out the *acting* bit.

There was a shuffle of feet behind Lukeson and Rochester.

'You're ruinin' business,' the barmaid complained. 'Your kind are about as welcome here as a Tory at a miners' do.'

Lukeson produced a photograph of the woman in the park. 'Have you seen this woman?'

94

'Gawd! Not looking like that I haven't. Poor cow. She been in an accident?'

'Strangled,' Lukeson said bluntly.

'There was a woman found dead in Layman's Park this mornin'. Is that — ?'

'Yes.'

'Poor cow,' she said again, with genuine feeling. Then, recovering: 'What's it got to do with me?'

'I'm sure nothing at all,' Lukeson said. 'We think she might have been in here last night.'

'It was jam-packed last night,' she said evasively. Unlucky for her, but luckily for Andy Lukeson, the barmaid did not have a natural liar's face.

Sensing that she was holding back, he said, 'Out with it.'

'Out with what?'

'Whatever it is you're holding back.'

'I ain't holding nothin' back,' she protested.

'Obstructing the police in an inquiry, and particularly a murder inquiry, is not looked on kindly or treated lightly,' he cautioned.

'Don't take much for you lot to wave the big stick, does it,' she complained. Lukeson waited. 'Yeah. She was in here.'

'Why did you say she wasn't?'

'Simple. I don't want no trouble.'

'So she was here. And?'

'There was a bit of a dust-up,' the barmaid said, after agonizing. 'Nothing out of the ordinary, right. There's hardly a night when there's not. It's the mix, ain't it. Drunks, prosses and punters. Like lighting matches in an explosives factory.'

'Dust-up?'

'One bloke, I think he was with her, goes to the loo. Another bloke sees a chance and moves in. Like I said, nothin' to write home about in a place where there's more horny toads than you'd find in a Florida swamp.'

'And what was the upshot of this,' Lukeson smirked, 'light entertainment?'

The barmaid shrugged. 'Fizzled out like most of 'em do.'

'And the men. Can you describe them for me?'

'Heads. Arms. Legs. Like ev'ryone else. After a while pullin' pints, it's all a blur. Godzilla could walk in here and I wouldn't notice. Know what I mean?' she asked Helen Rochester, having obviously decided that she was not going to get any sympathy from Lukeson.

'Am I suppose to believe that?' he said sternly. 'A sharp-eyed girl like you.'

'See these.' The barmaid pointed to bloodshot eyes. 'New contacts, giving me gyp. Got 'em three days ago. Wore them for an

96

hour and had to leave them out since. Move a couple of feet away, and you'll be in the middle of a fog that would shut down an airport. And if you don't believe me,' she said when Lukeson was openly sceptical, 'I'll give you the name of the specialist I had to go see this mornin'.'

The door behind the bar opened again and a man came through. 'Oh, dear, dear,' he groaned. 'I'll be blowed if it ain't Sergeant Lukeson. Oh, no,' he said with mock contrition. 'Inspector Lukeson now, ain't it?' He sneered. 'Well, for the time being, 'til Jack Porter's dicky ticker settles down again.'

The up-to-date nature of Ron Barkin's information showed how close he had his ear to the ground. Or, more worryingly, how efficient his line into Loston nick was.

Barkin let his small rat's eyes slide over Helen Rochester.

'Don't believe I've had the pleasure,' he said, his voice thick with innuendo.

'I doubt if knowing you would be a pleasure,' Rochester quipped.

'Ooooh. Touchy,' Barkin snorted. 'Thought you lot had to get to your coffins before first light.'

Ron Barkin's face, nose and ears were proof positive of how ill-equipped and how foolish he had been to think that he could have become a pugilist. He had spent three pain-filled years being beaten to pulp before he'd scraped together enough to buy the grungy pub, called the Whistler Inn, that had become the Coachman's Inn. Nothing much had changed except the name.

'Have you seen this woman, Barkin?' Lukeson proffered the photograph he'd just shown to the barmaid.

'Never set eyes on her,' Barkin said, looking to the ceiling.

'She was in here last night.'

Barkin shot the barmaid an annoyed look. 'Lotsa people are in here ev'ry night.'

'It's about that murder in Layman's Park, Ron,' the barmaid said, in her defence.

Barkin leaned on the bar. 'Now what would a bird who got herself topped in the park have to do with us, Lukeson?'

'We'll take your CCTV tapes,' Lukeson said, and asked, when Barkin laughed, 'Did I say something funny?'

'You might say so,' he said. 'You see, I've got customers who ain't very keen on being photographed.'

'No CCTV?' Rochester enquired sceptically.

Barkin pointed to a single camera above the bar angled to monitor the cash register, its only security function. 'This is a sticky fingers sort of business,' he said. 'What's Ron's should come to Ron, and that's all that worries me.' He glanced sideways at the barmaid. 'You'd be surprised how many employees believe in profit sharin', Inspector. One for you, one for me, know what I mean? Now, I'm real busy.' Barkin picked up a bar cloth and gave his full attention to wiping the bartop that did not need cleaning, marking, as far as he was concerned, the end of the interview.

'Know a man called Robbo Crabby?' Lukeson asked.

Barkin hunched his shoulders. 'Should I?'

'This is his local.'

'It's a lot of people's local.'

'Why do I get the feeling that you're telling me porkies, Barkin.'

'You're a copper. Must be your suspicious nature.' He turned to Rochester. 'If you ever get pissed off of hangin' round with arseholes, darlin', there's always a job here for you.'

'Oh, the blokes I work with are only little arseholes, Mr Barkin,' Rochester said sweetly. 'You're much too big an arse-hole to make the transition.'

'That'll be ten quid, Inspector,' he said sourly.

Lukeson took a ten pound note from his pocket.

'You're not going to pay him, Andy?' Rochester asked disbelievingly.

'Got to, girlie,' Barkin sniggered. 'Wouldn't look good for a copper to have walked out without coughin' up.' Andy Lukeson placed the ten pound note on the bar. 'Ta. Drop by any time, Inspector.'

Turning to leave, the door of the ladies' opened and a woman emerged, her smile instant and warm for Lukeson. 'Andy Lukeson,' she greeted him warmly, hugging him. 'It's been a while.' Although the rougher edges of a brogue had more or less been eradicated, there was still no doubting the woman's Irishness.

'How are you, Bridie?' Lukeson asked, with as much camaraderie as she had shown.

'Shouldn't that be how's tricks?' Barkin said, referring to the middle-aged woman's obvious profession.

'Shut it, Barkin!' Lukeson snapped.

'Don't you take any notice of him, Andy, me love,' Bridie said. 'Can't help it, you see. He was born outta the wrong end.' Her hearty laugh ended in a bout of bronchial coughing. She leaned on Lukeson for support. 'It's all that English soot that's got in me lungs,' she joked, when she got her breath back.

'That cough needs a doctor's attention,

Bridie,' Lukeson said, genuinely concerned.

'How ever do you put up with him?' Bridie enquired good-humouredly of Helen Rochester. 'Always fussing.'

Rochester returned her smile. 'To tell you the truth, it's a bit of an ordeal.'

Andy Lukeson chuckled. 'Oh, do feel free to gang up.'

'Oh, shit!' Bridie swore, looking to where the dark-haired man had been sitting waiting, but there was no rancour in her voice. 'You've buggered me lunch, Andy. He'd have been quick and easily pleased, too.'

'Sorry, Bridie.'

'Ah, don't worry, me love.' Her sigh was world weary. 'There's always another one along.'

Helen Rochester looked to Lukeson, curious about the obvious history between the woman and him, unlikely as it seemed.

'Bridie Murphy, meet Helen Rochester,' Lukeson said.

'To answer the question on your face, young one,' Bridie said, 'me and your boss have never done business, if that's what you're thinking.'

'I . . . I . . . I . . . '

'Good God, girl, you sound like an auld engine trying to get going on a frosty morning.'

Helen Rochester looked to Andy Lukeson for support, but all she got was a whimsical grin in return. He was enjoying her discomfort.

'Your boss is me own guardian angel, lovey.'

'It's been a while. How've you been keeping, Bridie?' he enquired.

'Ah, I'm holding together, Andy, boyo. Been in hospital with the bronchitis. I welcomed the rest.' She chuckled. 'And the bed to meself for a change. What're ye doing hanging out in a dive like this?'

'Bridie . . . ' He took the dead woman's photograph from his pocket, warning, 'This is not pretty. But might you have seen this woman around?'

'Indeed I have,' Bridie Murphy said instantly. 'But she was a whole lot better looking then.'

'When was then, Bridie?'

'Last night. Right here. Well, outside of here actually.'

'Sure?'

'Positive. There was a bit of a barny going on. Two fellas fighting over her, I think.'

'What time was that?'

'Oh . . . I was on me way back to me flat. Business was slow, you see.' She sighed wearily. 'At my age, business gets slower by the day. So that would be some time 'round eleven, maybe a bit later.'

'These men, can you describe them?'

'Not good enough to make a difference in a court of law, if that's what you want, Andy.'

'Just tell me what you saw, Bridie.'

'One was well set up — '

'Well set up?' Rochester queried.

'Went to the gym a coupla times a week, I'd say. Close-cut hair. Wore a dark overcoat, expensive.' She laughed. 'You get an eye for detail in my line of work. Could tell you almost to the penny how much a punter's got in his pocket,' she told Rochester. 'Soft-hands type.'

'Professional?' Lukeson asked.

'Clerkish,' Bridie concluded after consideration.

'And the other man?'

'Seen better times. Wore this great long yellow scarf.' Recalling the yellow wool thread found snagged on a bush at the crime scene, Lukeson's interest was immediate. 'Longish hair. Arty. When I looked back, the scarf was on the ground.

'Height?'

'Not much 'tween 'em. Close-cut hair was, I'd say, over six feet, six three, maybe. The other fella an inch or two shorter. But that's just an impression, lovey,' Bridie Murphy cautioned. 'I was at the other end of the street, you see. There's a street light just outside. That could be a help or a hindrance, depending on the shadows them things make.'

'Which one won the argument?' Rochester asked.

'Neither. She pitched both of them to blazes.'

'Neither man followed her?'

Bridie Murphy shrugged. 'I went on me way.'

'Did these men come out of here?'

'Can't say for sure. But the woman was tipsy, so I suppose they did.'

That tied in with the barmaid's story of a dust-up in the pub the previous night.

'Thanks, Bridie,' Lukeson said. 'You've been a great help.'

'What would they say back in the auld sod, boyo. Bridie Murphy, a true republican, helping an English copper with his inquiries. 'Twould send people spinning in their graves, I can tell you.'

Andy Lukeson took a second ten-pound note from his pocket to give to Bridie Murphy.

'Don't go insulting me now,' she said, pushing his hand away.

'Compensation. For the loss of your lunch.'

Andy Lukeson pushed the note into her hand again, and this time she took it.

'You know, Andy me love, you're not half bad for a bloody Englishman. Must have a drop of Irish blood in you from somewhere. I'll be on me way so.' She hugged Lukeson. 'You take care now, boyo. Them streets are bad places nowadays. And for heaven's sake, stop hanging round dives like this.'

'Clear off, you smelly old cow!' Barkin roared.

Lukeson turned angrily.

'Leave him be, Andy,' Bridie said. 'Sure dogshit like that isn't worth the bother.'

'One more thing . . . '

Bridie Murphy cackled bronchially. 'That's like something a punter would say.'

'Would you be willing to pop along to the station?'

'Ah, Andy. Me and police stations don't mix. It would be like adding sewer water to good malt. What would you want me round at the station for anyway?'

'To try and match the description of the men you saw arguing outside of here last night with what we've got. Or maybe work up an E-Fit.'

'Sure all I really seen was two fellas in the distance.'

'You described them fairly well for two

fellas in the distance, Bridie. We've got computer wizardry now. Bits and pieces can be brought together like magic, and before you know it — '

'Punters get worried when a pro goes to a cop shop, Andy.' Her blotched face clouded with fearful worry. 'Some might even drop by to ask about what you've been saying.'

Andy Lukeson knew well the dangers of the twilight world of the prostitute and her clients, a world that at any moment could erupt in terrible and often deadly violence.

'Why don't we get someone with a laptop to pop round to your place,' Helen Rochester suggested. 'Nice and private and very quietly.'

Bridie Murphy wavered.

'It really would help, Bridie,' Lukeson said.

'Yeah . . . well . . . just for you, mind,' she told Lukeson. 'But check first. I might be busy, you understand.'

'You keep safe, Bridie.'

Bridie Murphy looked at Lukeson as if he were an absolute innocent. 'I'm forty-two, looking sixty-two, lovey. Lots of young ones out there with firm boobs and well-shaped bums. An old sack like me can't be choosy no more.'

Bridie Murphy left.

'You give her a hard time, Barkin, and I'll make your life a misery,' Lukeson threatened.

Helen Rochester wondered why Lukeson was so protective of the middle-aged prostitute. But unless he was willing to say, she would not ask. Sometimes in police work, as in life, a shut mouth was better.

Leaving, Helen Rochester had an idea.

'Robbo Crabby said to say hello,' she called to the barmaid.

Her reaction, as Rochester had hoped, was instinctive. 'Cheeky sod, Robbo. Always trying to get in your knickers.'

Andy Lukeson gave his sergeant an admiring glance, at the same moment that the barmaid realized her gaffe. She shot Rochester a venomous look.

'Was he in here last night?' Rochester quizzed the barmaid, and when she did not answer, added, 'I'll take that as a yes, shall I? Had Crabby any contact with the murdered woman?'

'Might have chatted a bit,' the barmaid conceded grudgingly.

'Was Crabby one of the men in the argument outside?'

'I ain't Robbo's keeper!'

'But you'd like to be, wouldn't you,' Rochester said.

'Wouldn't do any good if I did. Robbo Crabby's a free spirit. Likes to put it about, does Robbo,' she said bitterly.

'We're a pub,' Barkin growled. 'Not a bloody kindergarten. What our customers get up to 'tween themselves is none of our business.'

Helen Rochester ignored his outburst. 'In what way did the woman respond to Crabby?' she enquired of the barmaid. 'Was she friendly? Gave him the heave-ho?'

'Hoity-toity. Look at me, ain't I the bee's knees.'

'What was Crabby's reaction?'

'Didn't bother him. Robbo's a trier. Not the knock 'em dead type.'

'Was Crabby wearing a yellow scarf?' Rochester asked.

'Don't be daft. Scarves are for ponces, ain't they.'

'Pleasant sort, is he, Crabby?' Lukeson enquired.

'Dunno what you mean?'

'No tendency towards violence when you were with him?'

'I never — ' the barmaid began, but let her protest die.

'A bit of a temper?' Lukeson said. 'Maybe if things don't go according to plan. His plan.'

The barmaid glared sullenly at Andy Lukeson.

'Look, putting it about as Crabby does, you

don't owe him any favours, do you?' Rochester empathized.

'No, do I?' the barmaid said bitterly, woman to woman. 'Yeah, if he gets too much beer in his belly, Robbo can be a narky one.'

'Take what's not on offer, maybe?' Helen Rochester prompted.

'Yeah. Sometimes.'

⋆ ⋆ ⋆

Getting into the car, Lukeson said, 'You did very well in there, Helen.' He phoned in for a check on Robbo Crabby. 'Might as well do one on Mel Burnett also.' When he broke the connection, he told Rochester, 'Crabby's been done twice for kerb crawling, and once for beating up on a prostitute. Burnett's clean.'

'A word with Robbo, I reckon,' Helen Rochester said.

⋆ ⋆ ⋆

Ten minutes later, Mel Burnett opened the door of her flat and, on seeing Lukeson, complained: 'Not you again. I've told you all I know.'

'We'd like to speak to Mr Crabby,' Lukeson said.

109

'Robbo? Why?'

'Just a word.'

'Well, you can't have no word, 'cause he ain't here.'

'When will Mr Crabby be back?'

'Gawd knows. Out of the blue, Robbo came off the sick and went back to work.' She snorted. 'Proves there's miracles, don't it.'

'Does he have a mobile phone?'

'Don't have it with him.' She pointed to a mobile phone on a hall table. 'Strange thing, he never leaves without it. In fact, he's hardly ever off the bloody thing. Can't imagine what people did before mobile phones were invented.'

'In a hurry, was he?' Helen Rochester enquired.

'For a lazy sod, yeah.' She studied Lukeson. 'What's all this 'bout anyway?'

'The name of his employer?' Helen Rochester asked.

'Ain't got one. Not a regular one. Robbo makes or gets a phone call, and that's his next job.'

'Cash in hand? Doesn't like paying taxes to HM's government, eh?' Rochester said.

'Don't know nothin' about that,' Mel Burnett said defensively.

'I think you know a lot more than you're willing to say, Ms Burnett,' Lukeson said.

'Now, are you sure you don't know who Mr Crabby is working for?'

Mel Burnett averted her gaze from Lukeson's. 'Ain't really sure.'

'But?'

'When Robbo was on the blower he was talking to Frank. I reckon that would be Frank Hancock.'

'And he is?'

'Owns a haulage outfit on the Brigham Road. Can't think of its name, but it's not far from the ridin' school. Has a great big flash of lightning on the side of its lorries. There won't be no trouble, will there?' Mel Burnett asked worriedly. ''Cause me and Lucy ain't ready to skip yet. Bein' shacked up with Robbo Crabby ain't me life's ambition, you understand.'

Andy Lukeson clapped himself on the back for his earlier shrewd reading of Mel Burnett's halfway house relationship with Robbo Crabby.

'Were you home last evening, Ms Burnett?' Rochester enquired.

'Yeah.'

Lukeson noted that Burnett seemed genuinely puzzled by Rochester's question.

'All evening?'

'I have a young kid. Don't get out much.'

'Didn't go out at all?'

'No.'

If Lukeson were a betting man, he'd give good odds that Mel Burnett was telling the truth.

'Was Mr Crabby with you?'

'Robbo ain't no homebird. More a B&B man, is Robbo Crabby.'

'So he was out?'

'Didn't I just say so,' Burnett replied narkily.

'At what time did he go out?' Rochester questioned.

'I got better things to do than watch the clock.'

'About.'

'Oh . . . half nine. That's the best I can do.'

'And he returned when?'

'Don't know. I was fast asleep.'

'At what time did you go to bed?'

'Round midnight.'

'And do you know where Mr Crabby went?'

'That's easy. Went down the pub.'

'What pub would that be?'

'Robbo's got an almighty thirst. So he wouldn't go far.'

'The Coachman's Inn, perhaps?'

'Yeah. That would be about Robbo's distance, all right.'

'Thank you, Ms Burnett.'

'Here, wait up,' she called after Lukeson and Rochester. 'What's Robbo suppose to have done?'

'We don't know that he's done anything,' Lukeson said.

'Don't give me that. You wouldn't be round here if he was a saint, now would ya.' She fixed Lukeson with a stare. 'It ain't nothin' to do with the woman in the park, is it?'

'Why should you think that?' Rochester asked.

'No reason, really,' she said, obviously regretting her question and anxious to initiate damage limitation.

Rochester held Burnett's gaze. 'Did Mr Crabby know the dead woman?'

'How would I know. Fact is, Robbo knows a lot of women. Seems he's got some kind of appeal for the ladies.' She snorted. 'Can't say what. I ain't never seen it. Look,' Mel Burnett began exasperatedly. 'Robbo's a lot of things, light-fingered and quick-fisted. And he ain't no gent. Rough as bloody sandpaper, in fact. But he ain't no killer! You're barkin' up the wrong tree if you think Robbo's done for that woman.'

Mel Burnett's was a desperate attempt to reassure herself, rather than convince Lukeson and Rochester.

On leaving the block of flats, Andy

113

Lukeson spotted a traffic camera at a junction where Vine Street joined a main road. The camera was set to monitor traffic approaching the junction along Vine Street going towards the junction. 'Get on to Traffic, Helen.' He pointed. 'What that camera saw might be of interest.'

'I doubt it,' Rochester opined, looking along the street. 'It's a long way off, Andy. And it seems to be angled mainly to keep tabs on vehicles in close proximity to the junction.'

'The Coachman's Inn can be reached from either direction, Helen. Admittedly the route going towards the junction is the longer, but there's a chance that it might have been favoured. If Mel Burnett went out last night, I want to know.'

'Do you really think that she — '

'Not really, I suppose,' Lukeson admitted honestly. 'But we're looking for a killer, and we're at the clutching any straw in the wind stage of the investigation.'

'I'll get on to Traffic.'

8

Hamlet's Rest, the Lamplin house, was situated in a leafy cul-de-sac, and it was a match of the other handful of residences on the road as Speckle and Johnson drove past, glimpsed through well cared for trees. Being a gardening expert paid very well indeed. However, Sally Speckle suspected that most of the money it would take to reside so exclusively was old money, and the considerable monies Lamplin had accumulated from his books had added to, rather than made, his fortune.

'Who is it?' the woman who answered DC Charlie Johnson's intercom summons asked sharply, and her sharpness of tone became sharper still when Johnson announced himself and the purpose of his visit, 'Go away. I have nothing more to say.'

'I have my superior, DI Speckle, with me,' Johnson said. 'She'd like a word, Mrs Lamplin.'

'I don't care if you have the Chief Constable with you. Go away!'

'Charming,' Johnson muttered.

'I heard that, Constable!'

Speckle shot Charlie Johnson a look of annoyance. 'Mrs Lamplin, there are some aspects of the burglary of your home I need to clarify,' she said in a no-nonsense fashion.

'Clarify?' A note of concern had replaced Cecily Lamplin's arrogance. 'I can't imagine what those aspects could possibly be, Inspector.'

'If you'll let us in, I'll explain, Mrs Lamplin.'

'Well . . . I haven't got much time.'

'Hopefully my enquiries won't take much time.'

The electronically controlled gates swung open.

Cecily Lamplin was on her mobile when they arrived at the house, marching agitatedly back and forth across the expansive circular forecourt, ignoring Speckle and Johnson when they got from the car. When they got closer, she swung round and proffered the mobile to Speckle. 'My husband would like a word.'

'Speckle, I presume,' Rupert Lamplin barked rudely when she spoke.

'You wished to speak to me,' she answered with admirable calm, though by now seething.

'*Tell* you, Inspector, would be a more precise term,' Lamplin replied in a clipped voice. In her mind's eye she could see Lamplin with his hand in his blazer pocket in the traditional aristocratic prat manner when forced to speak to a serf.

'*Tell* me what, sir?' Speckle responded stiffly.

'That you're making a nuisance of yourself, of course.'

'I'm afraid I could not agree, sir.'

'I don't care if you agree or not,' Lamplin rasped. 'My wife — '

'Reported a burglary,' Speckle interjected. 'And it's the job of the police to investigate her complaint fully and with all haste.'

'I can't see how harassing her helps.'

'Harassing? Indeed not. But we are pursuing our enquiries of a complaint by Mrs Lamplin. Would you have it any other way, Mr Lamplin?'

'A theft has taken place. Go find the thief. Simple as that.'

'We'll do our best, Mr Lamplin. But I need to check again what exactly happened.'

'I'm not sure I understand, Inspector.' There was distinct slippage in Lamplin's *back-in-your-box* attitude of a moment before.

'For security reasons, I'd prefer not to discuss this matter over the phone, Mr Lamplin.'

'Ah . . . yes. Indeed. Would you put my wife back on, please, Inspector.'

Speckle handed the phone back to Cecily Lamplin, who listened intently before murmuring a compliant: 'Yes, darling.' She broke the connection. 'Rupert thinks it best if he contacts our solicitor and comes home himself, Inspector. He would appreciate it, if your questions could wait until then.' Cecily Lamplin hurried back inside. Speckle and Johnson returned to her Punto to wait.

'Well, well,' Johnson said, settling in the passenger seat. 'Our visit seems to have stirred something of a hornet's nest.'

'Indeed, Charlie,' Speckle said thoughtfully. 'Indeed.'

★　★　★

'Can we drop by my flat and then the Post Office?' Helen Rochester requested of Andy Lukeson. 'A pressie I must send to my favourite aunt for her birthday. I should have posted it days ago. If I don't do it today it will be late.'

'What's an Acting DI for, if not to act as an unpaid chauffeur to his Acting DS,' Lukeson said, with sarcasm that was too exaggerated to be genuine. 'Tamworth Square it is then.' He went to take a sharp right.

118

'Ogilvie Street, actually.'

Lukeson braked without due care, forcing a delivery van behind him to take evasive action, just barely avoiding a fender bender. It went past, horn blaring. The driver's remark, unheard, lost nothing in muteness.

'Ogilvie Street?' Lukeson queried.

'The loo kept bunging up in Tamworth Square.'

'You should get a mortgage. Get your own place. You're getting on, you know.'

'Me? What about you? Within spitting distance of forty and you've been in the same flat for the last fifteen years.'

'Thirteen. And it's different for a man.'

'It always is, isn't it.'

'No flat, no post, unless you button it.'

'Talk about bullying in the workplace.'

'Take it or leave it, Acting DS Rochester,' he said loftily.

'Men,' Rochester grumbled good-humouredly. 'Couldn't God have come up with something better. Something with less nuisance value.'

'Don't push it,' Lukeson said, equally good-humoured.

Ten minutes later, auntie's present ready to be popped into a padded envelope, Lukeson pulled up outside the Post Office. Nudging the kerb, the book on Rochester's lap slid to the floor. The title of the book was: *Gardens*

To Die For by Rupert Lamplin.

'Is it damaged?' Lukeson asked concernedly.

Rochester checked, turning over the back of the book. 'No damage done.'

'Is that the Lamplin of the Loston Orchid Festival?' Lukeson asked, indicating the photo of an almost completely bald man on the back cover of the book, smoking a pipe.

'That's him. A bit of a legend in things green.'

'Looks like a Nazi camp commandant to me.'

'He's as austere as he looks,' Rochester said. 'Went to last year's Orchid Festival, which is Lamplin's brainchild, to get a copy of his last book signed for my aunt. He refused. Simply refused.'

'And you bought his book?'

'Aunt Harriet would take a book by Lamplin in preference to gold bars. She spends most of the day in the garden. Worrying, because she had a bit of a wobble a couple of months ago.'

Lukeson concentrated his gaze on the photograph of Rupert Lamplin, 'Looks familiar.'

'Probably saw him on telly sometime.'

'Don't watch gardening shows. Couldn't tell an orchid from a weed.'

She popped the book in the padded envelope. 'Won't be a tick, Andy.'

★　★　★

The gleaming red Jaguar roared up the drive, crunching gravel. The portly man who got from the car cast a hooded glance towards the Punto.

'At a guess, the Lamplin legal eagle,' Charlie Johnson observed.

Cecily Lamplin came from the house to greet him. A frenetic conversation ensued, with more hooded glances towards the Punto.

'Don't you fret, Cecily,' he was saying as Speckle and Johnson got from the car. 'I'll soon have all of this nonsense sorted. Speckle?' he enquired of Johnson, arrogantly assuming that the male of the pair would carry the senior rank. He was taken aback for a moment, but only for a moment, when Speckle responded. 'Ross. The Lamplin solicitor. Now what's all this about, Inspector?'

'As I've explained to Mr and Mrs Lamplin, my colleague and I are here to clear up some oddities with regard to the theft which — '

'I know all about that,' he interjected. 'Oddities, you say?'

Unlike the showy arrival of the Jaguar, a

Mercedes swept majestically up the drive. 'Darling,' Cecily was already calling out before Rupert Lamplin got from the car. She immediately sought the comfort of his arms, which he gave unstintingly. He kissed her on the forehead and turned his attention to Speckle. 'As you can see, my wife has been rather upset by your visit, the purpose of which had better have more to it than mere annoyance value.'

DI Sally Speckle held Rupert Lamplin's gaze, refusing to flinch as he obviously had anticipated that she would. 'As I have been explaining to your solicitor, Mr Lamplin, there are certain — '

'Oddities,' the solicitor snorted derisively.

Lamplin shot him a look that he would have given a mess on the sole of his shoe. The solicitor shrivelled as a bud experiencing the first winter frost might.

' — which need to be cleared up,' Speckle said.

'Such as?' Lamplin queried.

'Well, for one thing, the ease with which the thief gained access to the house.'

'Luck, Inspector,' Lamplin stated. 'That's what the wretch had. Here's what happened, in a nutshell, as explained already to the police. My wife and I were going to the opera — Verdi — Cecily's favourite composer. She laid out the evening frock she would be wearing on the bed in our bedroom. She placed the stolen necklace and tiara beside it while she showered. On her way back from the shower, passing a landing window, she saw a stray dog creating havoc in a rose bed she had newly planted. She went into the garden to put to rights the dog's rummaging, unfortunately leaving the patio doors open. The thief saw her go into the garden. Saw the patio doors open, and grabbed his good fortune. Damage repaired, Cecily went back upstairs and discovered the theft. What you're looking for, Inspector, is a sneak thief. And I'm sure that a check of your records will point you in the right direction. As I understand it, thieves are, in the main, slaves to a certain way of doing things.'

'Modus operandi, Inspector,' Ross intoned. 'There's the key.'

'Precisely,' Lamplin said.

'The idea is that access to the house was by way of the patio — '

'Oh, for God's sake, Inspector,' Rupert Lamplin barked. 'It's all so bloody obvious what happened here.'

Unfazed, Sally Speckle continued. 'I can't agree. How would the thief have known the patio doors were open? He saw them open, would be the obvious answer. However, the house is set well back from the road, Mr Lamplin, hidden by trees. The thief would have to have an eagle's eye.'

'Then go and find an eagle-eyed thief,' Lamplin snapped.

How Speckle was remaining calm in the face of such a belligerent prat, Charlie Johnson was at a loss to understand. He admired her calmness — at least, he suspected, what was her outward calmness.

'I put it to you, Mr Lamplin,' she went on. 'That it would be next to impossible for the thief to have seen the open patio doors. And, being aware, from her statement to DC Johnson of Mrs Lamplin's out of the way position in the garden, it would be equally unlikely that the thief could have seen her, or she him. There would also be the possibility of a dog or dogs to take in to account, CCTV, and also the risk of someone else being in the house. He or she was not to know that there were no dogs. Neither would a burglar expect to find a house of this nature without CCTV protection. That's quite a catalogue of risk for the thief, don't you think?'

'He was obviously watching the house, Inspector,' Ross said.

'Where from, Mr Ross? The house is situated at the end of a cul-de-sac, a distinct disadvantage to any thief who'd be of a mind to hang about. And, of course, although this house does not have CCTV, on my way here I observed several properties which had.'

Ross was stumped.

'There are plenty of tall trees from which the thief could have watched,' Cecily Lamplin said rather desperately.

'Trees have to be climbed, Mrs Lamplin. And to attempt to do so would only have made any thief even more conspicuous. I'm sure that someone would have called the police. I would suggest that, taking into account the risks involved, this robbery was not opportunistic as you think it was. Now, as I said at the outset, old ground needs to be gone over.'

'Do I have to make a complaint to be rid of you, you silly woman!' Lamplin bellowed, ignoring his solicitor's gesture for restraint.

'As a member of the public, making a complaint is your right, Mr Lamplin,' Speckle said, her tone of voice steely. 'I still have a job to do, which I fully intend doing, sir.'

DC Charlie Johnson had a grin that could only be described as smug.

Obviously not used to the lower classes standing on their hind legs, Rupert Lamplin glared at Sally Speckle in a desperate attempt to intimidate her. But she was not for turning.

'Can't you do something more useful than blather!' Cecily Lamplin demanded to know of Ross.

'Really, darling,' Lamplin said. 'You mustn't upset yourself.'

'Perhaps it would be better if you were to leave now and come back at another time, Inspector,' Ross suggested.

Speckle thought: and give you the chance to plug the holes in your client's story. Not bloody likely. She did not know what was going on, but her every instinct told her that more was being hidden than shown, unsaid than said.

'Can't really see the point of that, sir,' she replied.

'A dog with a bone, aren't you, Inspector,' Lamplin said.

'Only — '

'Doing your job,' he scoffed. He held Cecily to him. 'It's chilly out here. Shall we go inside?'

There was no mistaking the trepidation in Cecily Lamplin's eyes. He walked ahead, holding his wife as the strength seemed to leave her legs.

'I'll give you one thing, Inspector,' Ross said, going past. 'Your courage, if foolish, is admirable. One phone call from Rupert Lamplin and your career is over.'

'Much as I value your opinion, sir,' Speckle said, 'I'd rather you'd kept it to yourself. And should you try to intimidate me further, I'll not take kindly to it. Do you understand?'

Not finding a suitable riposte, Ross stormed off.

'That put the old bag of wind in his place, guv,' Johnson said. 'Wonder how much you'd have to be making in a year to own a Jag?'

'A great deal more than a detective constable,' Speckle said. 'And a great deal more than a detective inspector also.'

Sally Speckle walked ahead to the house.

'Lamplin will do you, if you give him half a chance,' Johnson warned Speckle, as he closed the front door behind him.

9

Andy Lukeson swung the car through the gates of the haulage company on the Brigham Road and came to a halt outside the Portakabin, a flash of lightning emblazoned on it, which served as an office. There was a shed to the rear of the yard where a mechanic was working on a lorry that looked as near to clapped out as didn't matter. He looked up disinterestedly, scratched his crotch and returned his attention to the lorry's engine, his demeanour suggesting that if he found the fault it would be by trial and error and a goodly measure of luck.

A barrel-chested runt of a man with ginger hair came from the Portakabin and shouted, 'I'll need that lorry on the road in an hour, Lenny.'

'Yeah. Yeah,' Lenny called back, in a manner that said: go screw yourself.

'One hour,' ginger-hair shouted back. 'Or you're out on your arse!'

'Not exactly the Rolls Royce of trucking, Andy,' Rochester observed. Ginger-hair focused on Lukeson and Rochester, immediate worry registering on his crumpled face. 'Now he's thinking what's the filth doing here? And cursing his luck that he hadn't taken greater care to hide the contraband.'

Ginger-hair did not bother being courteous; he turned away and went back inside the Portakabin, slamming the door shut behind him.

'Not a very friendly sort, is he,' Rochester said.

'Probably seen too many Sly Stallone movies. Shall we go and introduce ourselves?'

★　★　★

'Now, Mrs Lamplin,' DI Sally Speckle began. 'Just to run once more through the sequence of events as reported to DC Johnson.'

'Didn't he write it all down in his little notebook,' she said fretfully, her eyes darting to her solicitor from where no help was coming.

Charlie Johnson reckoned that Ross had lost his tongue because of Speckle's, unlike other officers, refusal to be brow-beaten. Being stood up to was something very new to the solicitor and it would take time to get used to.

'In your own time, Mrs Lamplin,' Speckle said.

'I was shopping. I came home about two

thirty. Made myself a cup of coffee. Ate a slice of apple tart. Washed the cup . . . ' Give me patience, Speckle thought. 'Well you did want every little detail, didn't you, Inspector,' she said, observing Speckle's frown of impatience. 'So I'm giving you every little detail.'

'I do, of course, deeply appreciate your unstinting cooperation, Mrs Lamplin,' Speckle said diplomatically. The '*but*' suggested in her statement did not need to be expressed.

Cecily Lamplin cast her eyes to the ceiling.

'Now, let me see . . . yes, I went upstairs to remove my make-up. While there, I laid out the clothes I would wear to the opera. Verdi, simply delightful. I also set aside the jewellery which I would wear.'

Cecily Lamplin was talking much too fast.

'The jewellery was to hand, then?'

'I'm not sure what you mean by *to hand*, Inspector?'

'What I mean is that one does not leave an antique diamond necklace and tiara lying about, does one?' Cecily Lamplin seemed stumped. 'Perhaps you have a safe in your bedroom?' Speckle queried.

Cecily Lamplin glanced to her husband.

'In my library,' he said.

'So you had to go downstairs to fetch the tiara and necklace, Mrs Lamplin?'

'Yes.'

'Has all of this a point, Inspector?' Ross asked.

'I think so,' Speckle said.

'How can my clients' domestic set-up be of interest? A theft has been committed and that's all that matters, surely.'

'I must admit that I, too, fail to see what relevance — '

'I don't think you do, sir,' Sally Speckle stated bluntly to Rupert Lamplin. 'Mrs Lamplin, what time was this?'

'I can't be sure.'

'I understand. An approximate time will suffice for now.'

'Inspector,' Ross groaned.

Speckle chose to ignore his intervention.

'Mrs Lamplin?'

'About three o'clock. Thereabouts.'

'And what time were you and your husband going to the opera?'

'Seven o'clock.'

'So you were leaving very valuable jewellery lying about for hours.'

'In hindsight, it was a very silly thing to do, of course.'

'It would appear to be, yes.'

'We've never been burgled before, so I suppose I had become complacent. One does, doesn't one. One gets a false sense of security.'

'Is it your normal practice to remove jewellery from the safe hours before wearing it?'

Cecily Lamplin touched her forehead. 'I have the most dreadful headache.'

'I think this has gone far enough, Inspector,' the Lamplins' solicitor said. 'Mrs Lamplin made a silly mistake and paid the price for it. Therefore she does not need to be stressed out further by . . . well, police waffle.'

'If you'll just bear with me for a while longer,' Speckle said.

'I think a word with your superior might be in order,' Ross threatened.

'That would be Chief Superintendent Doyle. Shall I give you his number, sir.'

The threat having failed, he murmured, 'Well, don't drag this out endlessly.'

'No longer than necessary,' Speckle said.

DC Charlie Johnson was in open admiration of Sally Speckle's refusal to be browbeaten. He was not at all sure that if it were he who was taking the flak that he'd have had as much resilience.

'So you went to the safe in your husband's study, got the jewellery, came back upstairs and placed it with the clothes you would be wearing to the opera, Mrs Lamplin?'

'Yes.'

'What happened next?'

'I took a shower.'

'And it was on your way back to your bedroom, while passing a landing window that you saw this dog you mentioned?'

'Yes,' she said angrily. 'A great hulking animal of uncertain pedigree, wreaking absolute havoc in a rosebed I'd only the day before replanted. Orchids are Rupert's love. Roses, mine. Though I've not come anywhere close to the wonderful success he has had.'

'What did you do then?'

'It's all in the statement I made to him!' Cecily Lamplin's pointed a quivering, accusing finger at DC Charlie Johnson. 'Didn't you read the bloody thing, woman?'

'You stated that you came back downstairs, and went outside to repair the damage.'

'Obviously you have read my statement, which only makes me wonder what you're doing here wasting my and your time, Inspector.'

'Indeed,' Ross intoned.

'Sometimes, after the dust has settled, little things come back to memory which are often, in police experience, the key to unlocking new avenues of investigation. Please go on, Mrs Lamplin. You put to rights the damage the dog had done.'

'My labours rendered my shower useless, so when I came back inside I went upstairs to shower again.'

'And that's when you discovered the theft of the jewellery?'

'And five hundred poun — ' Cecily Lamplin bit her tongue.

'Five hundred pounds?' Speckle checked. 'I saw no mention of this in DC Johnson's report, Mrs Lamplin.'

'That's because it wasn't reported in the statement,' Johnson said defensively.

'I'm sorry, Inspector. It slipped my mind.'

'You see the value of our chat now, don't you?' Speckle's eyes flashed from Cecily Lamplin to her husband.

'Five hundred pounds is a sizeable sum to have slipped your mind, don't you think?' Johnson questioned Cecily Lamplin, infuriated by her attempt to falsely drop him in it.

Cecily Lamplin looked with imperious haughtiness at Johnson. 'I dare say that to some it might seem so, Constable.'

'This five hundred pounds,' Sally Speckle said. 'Was it with the jewellery?'

'Ah . . . no. It was in a bedside locker.'

'Do you normally keep five hundred pounds in a bedside locker, Mrs Lamplin?'

'It was something I just stuffed in there in passing, Inspector.'

'Do you have domestic staff, Mrs Lamplin?'

'Domestics are like CCTV,' Cecily Lamplin

said. 'Only with ears to listen with and mouths to talk with.'

DI Sally Speckle could not help thinking that either Cecily Lamplin suffered from acute paranoia, or she had something to hide. It was the latter she was interested in.

'How many rooms are there in the house, Mrs Lamplin?'

'Rooms?'

'Yes.'

'In all?'

'Yes.'

'Would you like them listed individually or just a round number?' Cecily Lamplin enquired sarcastically.

'A round number will do, thank you.'

'Twenty-one.'

'A lot of rooms, isn't it,' Speckle murmured thoughtfully. 'In what part of the house is your bedroom situated, Mrs Lamplin?'

'In the east wing. Why? I can't imagine how the number of rooms in the house can be relevant to your enquiries, Inspector.'

DC Charlie Johnson thought that judging by Rupert Lamplin's bobbing Adam's apple, he was not as mystified.

'How long were you in the garden?' Speckle enquired.

'What's that got to do — '

'How long?' Speckle interjected.

'Not long. I just tidied up the rosebed, intending to return to it at another time.'

'Five minutes.'

'More.'

'Ten, then?'

'About that. Why?'

'Ten minutes for the thief to enter the grounds, taking due care, find a means of entry, and search the house, all twenty-one rooms of it,' Speckle emphasized. 'Not much time to do all that, wouldn't you say. In fact, given the time frame, the thief must have gone straight to your bedroom, wouldn't you say, Mrs Lamplin? Which might suggest that the thief knew where to find the jewellery. But then, in the first place, how would he or she have known where to look? Luck? If the thief had that kind of luck, when I find him or her, I'll ask them to pick my lottery numbers.'

Suddenly weary, Rupert Lamplin held her gaze. 'Where do we stand, Inspector?'

'Frankly, sir, I'm not inclined to believe the reported version of events,' Sally Speckle stated bluntly.

Lamplin exchanged looks with his wife and Ross, neither of whom had anything to offer. 'A word, Inspector?'

'Certainly, sir.'

Cecily Lamplin's plea was silent, but all the

more poignant for that. He squeezed her hand gently.

Charlie Johnson went to join Speckle.

'Alone, Inspector,' Lamplin requested. 'We can talk in my study.' He led the way to a room across the hall.

DC Charlie Johnson thought Lamplin's hairpiece ridiculous. In fact, as close to vaudevillian as didn't matter. The perspiration on his forehead, and no doubt under the toupee, had dampened its texture, and it looked as if Lamplin was walking about with a dead rat on his head.

10

'What do you lot want?' the ginger-haired man enquired narkily of Lukeson and Rochester when they entered the cramped Portakabin.

'Frankie Hancock, no less,' Lukeson said. 'Small world, isn't it.'

Hancock chuckled and cast an appreciative eye over Helen Rochester, the slimmer model (her battle with her weight a constant struggle, as she swung between the temptations of her sweet tooth, particularly a fondness for canteen cream cakes, and the latest carrot juice and lentils, or whatever diet offered hope at the time). 'Wouldn't half mind keepin' company with you, darlin'.' He settled his gaze on Andy Lukeson, as if he'd only then recognized him. 'Sergeant Lukeson.'

'Inspector Lukeson,' Rochester said.

'Inspector, eh. Sold out at last have you, Andy, lad? Next thing you know you'll be Chief Constable. Ain't had the pleasure of your company for a while.'

'Last time we met you were, as the jargon would have it, caught in possession. Counterfeit ciggies, as I recall.'

'Looked the real thing though, didn't they. The Turks could always make muck look like the business. But I get about less these days. All that subterfuge, nice word that, subterfuge. Learned it inside from a bloke who had degrees comin' out his bum, but couldn't keep his hands off old dears' savings. Gettin' too old to be hangin' round outta the way coves at dead of night.'

He massaged his left hip.

'Joints ain't what they used to be in the old days. Me old mum would be proud of me,' he waved a hand about, 'gone legit.' His laughter was surprisingly infectious, and was completely at odds with his previous sour-faced demeanour. 'Of course, me old man, may he rot in hell, would have taken me aside and laid in to me. Not much for the straight and narrow, was Frankie senior. Only one thing he'd have hated more than me goin' legit, and that was if I took to wearin' pink tights, know what I mean, darlin'?' he asked Rochester mischievously.

Hancock settled his gaze on Lukeson.

'So what kinda lorry would you like to hire, then?'

'The one stuffed with dodgy gear,' Lukeson returned.

Hancock was wide-eyed. 'Dodgy gear? Like I said, I've gone legit,' he protested, but with a twinkle in his eye.

'Oh, give it a rest,' Lukeson barked. 'When you get to hell you'll nick the coal!'

'No, I won't. There won't be any left. Me old man will've got the lot.'

'Robbo Crabby?'

'Robbo? Been a naughty boy, has he?'

'Where can we find him?'

'Oh, dearie, dearie. What's he been up to, that you want him so urgently?'

'You should know how the system works, Frankie,' Lukeson said. 'You've experienced it often enough. We ask the questions, you give the answers.'

'Touchy.' He nodded in Helen Rochester's direction. 'Ain't she givin' you any?'

'Just answer the Inspector's questions,' Rochester snapped.

'Ya know,' Hancock said, 'you could make a lot more pullin' punters than bein' a copper. But if you stick with bein' a mug, I'd ditch the civvies and don the uniform. I know a thousand blokes who dream 'bout beddin' a woman in uniform.' He chuckled. 'Better still if it's a copper bein' screwed.'

'You should gargle more, Frankie,' Lukeson said. 'It'll help keep your mouth clean. Now, Robbo Crabby,' he demanded to know.

'Don't see much of Robbo.'

Andy Lukeson leaned forward face to face

with Hancock. 'Frankie, how much time do you reckon you'll pull if I get a search team in here right now, eh?'

'Headed for Norwich,' Hancock said, pragmatically. 'A load of washin' machines. Legit,' he quickly added.

'We'll need the truck reg and the place where he's dropping this legit load.'

'No problems.' Hancock typed into a desktop computer. 'Print the lot out for ya. So that if you can't read, the girlie can read it for ya. Looks a bright thing, don't she.' And added as the computer was printing, 'Ain't prison wonderful nowadays. Learned all 'bout these beauties,' he tapped the computer, 'inside. Said it would help me get a job when I got out. They was right. Here I am, me own lord and master.'

'Very resilient machines,' Lukeson said. 'The way they can stand up to falling off the backs of lorries, Frankie.'

Hancock chuckled. 'Ain't your guv'nor the card, officer,' he said to Rochester. He tore off the printout and handed it to Lukeson. 'Nice seein' you again, Mr Lukeson. No offence. Don't mind if it's as long again.'

'What kind of man is Crabby?'

'He's a smiler.'

'A smiler?' Rochester checked.

Frankie Hancock shook his head. 'Ain't she

141

an innocent, eh, Lukeson.'

Rochester looked to Lukeson for clarification.

'A smiler means that Crabby would not be a nice man to get on the wrong side of, particularly in a dark alley,' he explained. 'Why do you employ him, Frankie? If, as you claim, you're legit.'

'Long haulers ain't easy to come by nowadays, Lukeson. Men now want to spend what the tossers call *quality time* with their birds and brats. Meaning they're lazy sods who only want to haul freight 'tween 9 and 5 and never at weekends. For that they want the crown bloody jewels.' He laughed. 'I'm a businessman. Gotta keep costs down, ain't I.'

'And Robbo Crabby likes to do a bit of business on the side, so you lay that off against pay, right?'

Hancock crossed himself. 'God forgive ya, Mr Lukeson. I never said no such thing.' He picked up a mug off the desk that had, by the amount of slime on it, last been washed during the war. 'Like a cuppa? Was just makin' one when you called.'

'You should toss that away,' Lukeson said, indicating the mug. 'Before you're nabbed under some public health law.'

'Never. This mug came all the way down from me gran.'

Which, Lukeson thought, gave veracity to the time which he had estimated since it had last been washed.

'Like women, does he, Crabby?' Lukeson asked.

'Don't we all, Mr Lukeson.'

'Don't beat about the bush, Frankie. I get impatient. And when I get impatient, I get curious,' Lukeson said pointedly.

'Should see someone about that,' Hancock said.

'And I get impatient and nasty if I'm pissed off!'

Hancock grinned. 'Yeah. From what I'm told, Robbo's fond of the ladies.'

'How fond?'

'Now how would I know!' Hancock frowned. 'Ain't nothin' I can say that's gospel, ya understand.'

'Oh, humour me with a bit of gossip then,' Lukeson said expansively.

'A time or two, so I've heard, Robbo's taken his pleasure . . . credit, you might say. Does that satisfy your impatience and curiosity, Mr Lukeson?'

'It goes a long way, Frankie.'

'Ya know, you ain't bad for a copper. Sure you won't have that cuppa?' Andy Lukeson looked at the filthy mug and shook his head. 'Pity.'

'I'll get Uniform round,' Helen Rochester said, once outside.

'To do what?'

'Search the place, of course, Andy.'

'Unless they get here within fifteen minutes, there won't be anything to find. Besides, Hancock is old school. Doesn't beat up on old ladies for their pensions, or flog poison to youngsters. There's bigger and much nastier fish in the pond than Frankie Hancock. And he's always come quietly when he's been rumbled.'

'Credit?' Rochester queried.

'Meaning, if the lady isn't willing, Robbo Crabby isn't adverse to taking what he wants anyway.'

'Seems Crabby isn't a nice man.'

'But is he a killer?' Lukeson said.

*　*　*

As he entered the study, Rupert Lamplin's right leg seemed to wobble under him, and he clutched the door for support.

'Are you all right, sir?' Speckle enquired.

'Polio when I was younger,' he explained. 'Nerves and muscles act up now and then.' He patted his leg, like the stereotype war veteran with shrapnel in his leg. 'Nothing to worry about, Inspector.' He closed the library

144

door, and went and sat behind a very impressive antique mahogany desk, gently massaging his right leg. 'Please sit.'

Sally Speckle sat, and waited while Lamplin got his thoughts in order, when he suggested: 'Perhaps a withdrawal of my wife's complaint would be best all round.'

'I'm not sure I understand, sir.'

Lamplin held Speckle's gaze. 'Oh, I think you do, Inspector. You're a very intelligent woman, not easily hoodwinked.'

'Your wife made the complaint, Mr Lamplin. Only she can withdraw it.'

'Cecily will do as I tell her.'

The sleeping feminist inside Speckle came awake. 'A withdrawal might be seen as wasting police time, Mr Lamplin.'

'I'll square all that.'

Goaded by his feudal attitude, Speckle dug her heels in. A moment ago she was more or less willing to be charitable and walk away, but not now. 'As the investigating officer, I'd much prefer if you squared it with me, sir. Then in turn, if necessary, I can square it with whoever it needs squaring with.'

'A dog with a bone, aren't you, Inspector.'

'I like to dot the t's and cross the i's, sir.'

Resigned, Lamplin asked, 'Can I rely on your absolute discretion?'

'Of course,' Speckle assured him, but

145

qualified, 'but only if that discretion does not compromise the law.'

Rupert Lamplin became introspective. It was a long time before he spoke. 'There's no thief, Inspector. There was no crime. But there was a theft of sorts.'

'Of sorts?'

Lamplin poured himself a stiff brandy. 'My wife is of . . . ' he swallowed most of the brandy in one gulp, ' . . . shall we say an adventurous nature, Inspector.'

Sally Speckle waited.

'She, ah . . . ' He thought deeply for a moment before obviously deciding on forthrightness as the best course. 'Simply stated, Cecily likes to pick up strange men.' Now, like a penitent having worked up the courage to confess, he rushed on: 'The man who took the jewellery and cash was one of a long line of such men.'

Though Rupert Lamplin was an obnoxious, arrogant man, DI Sally Speckle now had sympathy for what was clearly an ordeal for him.

'On the day in question, Cecily met this man on a bus.' His sigh was a world weary one. 'Pick-ups on buses are a particular favourite of hers. She went with him to an apartment she rents, but she quickly tired of him, left and came straight home. The man

146

followed her home.

'Her panic was understandable. However, his interest was not sexual. He wanted money. Good old-fashioned blackmail. They struck a bargain — the jewellery and £500. And that would have been that, had . . .' He puffed out his cheeks and let out a pent-up breath of exasperation. 'My wife controlled her peevishness, though understandable under the circumstances, and not acted in a decidedly stupid manner by reporting a theft to the police, wanting revenge on her blackmailer, not thinking about what would happen if the police caught him. Or if she got an investigating officer, like you, who could see the many flaws in her story and think again.

'I'm sure there'll be an issue about wasting police time, Inspector. For which I will have to beg your forgiveness and your indulgence. Despite her exterior brashness, inwardly my wife is a terrified woman. Living in fear of becoming an outcast from decent society were her idiosyncratic ways to become public knowledge.

'It would ruin her and break me, I fear.

'I still have hopes that one day one of the many psychiatrists and psychologists she sees will be able to unlock whatever drives her compulsion. Until then, I'm sincerely hoping that the family skeleton can remain firmly locked in its closet, Inspector.

'You have my sincere apologies for being so rude to you and your colleague. But such an approach has always worked in the past, and I foolishly thought it would do so again this time. Please forgive me.'

DI Sally Speckle was, as Rupert Lamplin hoped, an understanding officer. She decided that no good would come of doggedly pursuing the charge of wasting police time, with the risk that somewhere along the line a leak through error or intent would lay bare Cecily Lamplin's secret life. And besides, she had seen another side to Lamplin. He seemed genuinely concerned to protect his wife from scandal, and it could not be easy for him to have to share her with a string of strange men.

'I'll still need your wife to officially withdraw her complaint, Mr Lamplin.'

He sprang up and went to the door and opened it. 'Cecily, darling. Will you come here, please.' Cecily Lamplin came into the room, her eyes flashing wildly about like a cornered fox waiting for the kill. Lamplin tenderly took her hands in his, which she tried to pull away as if trying to flee, but he held her firm. 'The Inspector understands, my dear,' he said softly. 'Don't you, Inspector?' Sally Speckle nodded. 'There, you see, darling. There's no further need to fret. Everything will be all right. All you have to do is withdraw your silly complaint. Will you do that? For me.'

'Yes,' she murmured.

'Good girl. Now you go and wait for me, I shan't be long.' When she left, Lamplin said, 'I won't forget your understanding and kindness, Inspector. Perhaps one day we'll meet again in less fraught circumstances. Thank you.'

'Goodbye, sir.'

'Goodbye, Inspector.'

She paused before she left. 'Of course, you do realize that blackmailers nearly always return, Mr Lamplin.'

He drew in a long deep breath. 'Oh, yes. Indeed I do, Inspector.'

'What then?'

'He may also be run over by a bus, if I'm lucky,' he said wearily. 'We shall just have to wait and see. If he does come back, perhaps he won't be too unreasonable in his demands.'

'The police could help.'

'No. We'll muddle along, I dare say.'

'Has this been the first time your wife has been blackmailed?'

'Incredibly so, in the three years since this illness afflicted her, yes. We have been very fortunate. You'll understand that the fewer people who know about this, the better, Inspector.'

'You must love your wife very much, Mr Lamplin.'

'I do, Inspector.'

★ ★ ★

'Well?' DC Charlie Johnson asked a couple of minutes into the drive back to Loston nick, when he reckoned he had waited long enough for an explanation from Speckle. 'What was all that about?'

'Nothing much, really.'

'Nothing much? I'm not sure we're on the same wavelength here, guv.'

DI Sally Speckle pulled over and parked. 'Charlie, do you trust me?'

'Of course I trust you.'

'Trust me enough to believe me when I tell you that this whole matter is best left to die a death?'

Charlie Johnson thought for a long time before answering, 'Yes, ma'am.'

DI Sally Speckle put the car in gear and drove off, her thoughts on her lunch date with Simon Ambrose, thoughts which she found very pleasurable. And again, as she had often in the days since he had walked back into her life, she wondered if she was falling in love with him all over again. Did such things happen when you were thirty years old? And supposed to have acquired sense along the way.

'Thanks, Charlie,' she said. Her mobile rang. 'Would you, please.'

Charlie Johnson picked up her mobile perched on the dashboard. After his cheery greeting, he held the phone out for Speckle to take. 'A bloke.'

She pulled over again.

'Sorry about this, Sally,' Simon Ambrose said. 'Something's come up.' Speckle's disappointment was a sharp needle through her heart, until he added, 'Dinner instead. Same place.' He chuckled musically. 'And we can share the cost of a cab.' The needle through her heart became a giddiness in her head.

'Fine, Simon.'

'I look forward to it, Sally,' he said in a coaxing voice.

'Me, too. 'Bye.'

Driving on, DC Charlie Johnson wondered if the man on the phone was the one to cut inside Andy Lukeson. If he was, Lukeson had only himself to blame. It was the common opinion around Loston nick that had Andy Lukeson taken courage and moved, Sally

Speckle would not have turned him away.

Giving his guv'nor an appreciative sideways glance, he wished he'd been in Lukeson's shoes, stupid bastard.

★ ★ ★

Acting DI Andy Lukeson was getting into his car at the trucking company when his mobile rang. After announcing himself, he listened intently. 'When did this happen? Yes. Right away.' He got into the car urgently.

'What was that all about?' Rochester asked.

'Bridie Murphy.'

'Who?'

'The Irish woman I spoke to in the Coachman's Inn an hour ago. She's in Loston General, critically ill. She's been asking for me.'

'What happened?'

'Someone hit her with a blunt instrument and left her for dead.'

★ ★ ★

Andy Lukeson pulled into the car park of Loston General Hospital, frustrated and anxious at not seeing a car space free. On the trip over from the haulage company, Helen Rochester had checked twice on the condition of

Bridie Murphy. 'Holding on,' was the best that could be said. Time was obviously of the essence, and driving around the car park looking for a vacant space was not the best way to spend it. 'Over to you, Helen,' he said, braking. 'Follow me in.'

'Look,' Rochester pointed to where a young traffic officer was waving to them. He pointed to the side of the building, where he had presumably reserved a parking slot. Lukeson hurried inside, where a second uniformed officer was waiting to escort him to ICU.

The room was dim, the monitor screens seeming to hang in the air like distant planets of the universe. A medical team were in attendance, doing what they could, but their body language indicated that there wasn't much they could do. Lukeson introduced himself to the senior member of the team. Him being the oldest, Lukeson had automatically assumed that he was the highest-ranking clinician, but that turned out to be a fresh-faced woman in her early thirties.

'Not looking good,' she murmured. 'Severe head trauma. Coming and going. It's a miracle that she's alive at all.'

Lukeson took Bridie Murphy's hands in his and spoke softly, 'Hello Bridie, it's Andy Lukeson, my love.'

Tired, hopeless eyes flitted open, the lids much too heavy. She smiled. 'Hello, Andy, I'm done for, darling.' Lukeson thought about uttering words of reassurance, but thought better of it; he'd not fool her, and the spectre of death was everywhere. 'Thanks for not giving me a load of old bullshit about getting better.'

She beckoned him closer.

'I've got something to tell you, me lovely.'

Andy Lukeson grinned and squeezed her hand. 'And what might that be, you cute Irish colleen?'

She laughed feebly.

'Colleen? Me? Colleens are virginal maidens, Andy, not worn out old whores like me.' She glanced up at a monitor. 'Fancied I'd always kick the bucket back home,' she said sadly. 'Won't be long now before Gabriel blows his horn.' Her sigh was long and weary. 'You know, me lovely, I won't mind one little bit when he does.'

Conscious of precious seconds ticking away, Lukeson was still reluctant to press the Irishwoman for the information she had.

A nurse, sensing Lukeson's indecision and understanding the urgency, rubbed Bridie Murphy's arm. 'Sure won't you tell this fine Englishman what you have to tell him, Bridie, before he's old enough for his pension.' One

154

would not call the nurse's accent a brogue, if such ever existed outside a Hollywood studio, but the burr of certain words such as 'sure' formed a bond with the dying woman.

Bridie Murphy grabbed the young nurse's hand and urged: 'Go home, girl. Don't leave it too late, like me.' She looked at Andy Lukeson. 'Andy, me love, I know the name of the killer you're looking for. The one who done for that poor wretch in Layman's Park.' She went on breathlessly, a bright sharp glow in her eyes. 'Saw her. Tipsy, she was. I was coming out of an alley, call of nature. Crossing to the park, she was. Said she was foolish. Full of junkies and yobbos. But she wouldn't listen. I was getting into a punter's car when I saw the killer going into the park after her. But by then she'd gone off into the darkness.'

'Why didn't you tell me this earlier, Bridie?'

'I should have, me lovely. But, you see, I thought there'd be a couple of easy quid to be made.'

'Blackmail?'

'Don't sound so bloody righteous, Andy. I'm not in the bloom of life. I only pick up the dregs now, or men who fancy an auld one for some strange reason. And he's one of them strange ones.'

'You know this man?'

She grinned mischievously. 'Every inch of him, you might say. He called round to me flat. I'd have got on to you right after he'd left, when I had his money in me fist. But it all went wrong,' she said wearily. 'As wrong as it could, me lovely.'

'Who is this man, Bridie?' Lukeson asked urgently.

'His name is . . .'

11

Bridie Murphy went rigid, her mouth opening and closing, trying to speak, but only managing a horrible gurgling sound from deep within her. The monitors bleeped frantically. She looked strickenly at Lukeson and sank deep into the pillows, looking instantly smaller, a child with a wizened face. Lukeson was startled by the suddenness of her collapse and the stark change in her countenance. First pain and terror. Then a calmness that swept away all the pain.

'You'll have to leave now,' Lukeson was told.

'Is she — '

'No. Coma. But I doubt very much if she'll come out of it,' the senior clinician said. 'She'll pass away peacefully.'

The police officer took over in Lukeson. 'She didn't mention a name?' His eyes flashed round the medical team, to be met by shaking heads.

'She only came round briefly to ask for you,' the Irish nurse said.

Lukeson leaned over and kissed Bridie Murphy on the forehead. 'Thanks anyway, Bridie,' he said.

The small cramped and very grungy flat in which Bridie Murphy lived plunged Andy Lukeson's spirits lower than they already were. He had been here once before, years ago when he had seen Bridie home after a beating he'd prevented, which would probably have ended in her death. 'You should go to a hospital,' he'd advised her.

'Hospital?' she'd said cynically, through mushy, swollen lips. 'If I did that every time a punter beat up on me, I'd spend more time there than here.' She'd waved her hand over the tip that was her flat. 'You can't imagine how green Tipperary fields are.' Her gaze had been far away, in a time and place long since past.

Looking about him now, as then, Lukeson thought that it was indeed a long way to Tipperary.

'Anything?' Lukeson enquired of the SOCO team leader.

'It'll be a long haul,' he replied. Looking critically about the cramped, damp and unhygienic room, he added disgustedly, 'How can someone live like this?'

'Hopelessness,' Lukeson said.

'Hopelessness?'

'Yes. When you spend every day living in a

dream that one day that dream will come to pass. It's a story that's repeated a million times over in Irish clubs and pubs. The dream of one day returning home. For most, like the woman who lived here, it never happens. And as the dream fades, this,' he waved his hand over the grotty flat, 'happens.'

'It's just filth! Pure and simple.'

Andy Lukeson did not try to convince the SOCO. It would be a useless exercise, because thinking back, before he had met Bridie Murphy, gentle and much abused, his views would have been similar; views fashioned by a history of conflict and bitterness; dominion and enslavement; master and servant; a history that would last well into the future; a dangerous history that would take a very long time for the wrongs on both sides to be admitted to and set aside in a new beginning, each spasmodic lapse back into lunacy setting a new and far flung date for eventual reconciliation and a craved for peace by all men of goodwill.

'What would a pro want with that lot?' the SOCO asked scornfully, pointing to a shelf of books on the wall above a dark, partially dry stain on the threadbare carpet.

Lukeson recalled how, when he had seen Bridie Murphy home (on the night he had come to her rescue, fearing that were he to leave her to make her own way home, the man who had been kicking her like a football and had run away, would still be in the neighbourhood and renew his attack) he, like the young SOCO, had been astonished to find books, too, let alone the luminaries of literature, even a much thumbed *Taming of the Shrew*.

'You need a bit of an uplift after some of the arseholes I bring here,' Bridie had said, on seeing his surprise. 'A bit of Shakespeare is nice then. Joyce, too. And Oscar Wilde for wit and humour. But some bits are beyond me. The nuns in the orphanage were more into slave labour than fancy reading.'

'Tough, was it?' he'd asked.

'Got a bit easier when the nuns found that I had green fingers. Used to spend most of me time after that in the garden. And the grub for gardening was a bit better than the swill for working in the laundry. Even in orphanages there's rungs on ladders ... I don't know your name.'

'Andy.'

'You're not like the others, Andy,' she'd said. 'Never change, will you.'

Lukeson hoped he had not.

'An intellectual pro,' the SOCO snorted. 'What next?' His voice reeked of contempt. 'Being Irish, I can only assume that she had

160

punters who liked to read while screwing her.'

'Have respect,' Lukeson barked. 'And less of the racist claptrap!'

Lukeson's mobile rang.

'Norwich police have spoken to Crabby.'

'And?'

'He's got an alibi for the time of the murder, Andy,' Helen Rochester said. 'And a hell of a good reason for coming off the sick and returning to work.'

He listened with sinking spirits, spirits which dropped further with more bad news.

'And you were right about the Traffic CCTV at the junction of Vine Street, Andy. Gives a reasonable quality pic of the building where the Crabby flat is. It picked up Crabby leaving at 9.15. But no sign of Mel Burnett having left.'

'Maybe she just wasn't recognizable, Helen?'

'Not recognizable? You mean she was disguised?' she queried doubtfully.

'Well, if she had murder in mind, she could be aware of the CCTV at the junction and the part it might play. And Burnett is not lacking in intelligence.'

'A bit Golden Age detective story, that,' was Rochester's opinion.

'Telly is a great educator. Sometimes I think it's become a Home Study course for criminals. Go back over the footage, Helen,' he said, unnecessarily terse.

'You're the boss.'

'Yes, I am.' His apology was immediate. 'Sorry. We need to make a breakthrough, Helen. Desperate times makes for desperate measures.'

'You'll get the killer, Andy,' she said.

'Thanks for the vote of confidence. I just hope that it's justified,' he said glumly. 'I'll head over to Brigham.'

'Brigham?'

'Yes. Three years ago there was a woman called Sandra Fairweather murdered in Cobley Wood, the part that's on Brigham's patch. Strangled. The case went cold. A word with DI Alfie Blair, who headed up the investigation, probably won't lead anywhere, but you never know.'

★ ★ ★

Andy Lukeson could have picked up the phone and called Alfie Blair, but he had opted to drive to Brigham, needing time to think, and to hopefully shift the feeling that he would not solve the case, that the investigation was bogging down before slipping away altogether. It was a feeling that had no basis (because he had been involved in several murder investigations with Sally Speckle and a couple before her time, also, and he would say that he had played his part in bringing the killers to justice), but that made it nonetheless daunting. To draw an analogy with the theatre, this time he was not playing a part, he was playing the lead, and that was very far removed from being a minor player in the background.

Failure would be fairly and squarely his alone.

Robbo Crabby had been interviewed by the police and had been eliminated from his enquiries because he had provided an alibi that had been checked out and confirmed. The married woman he had been with, now in a battered wives refuge, had readily admitted to Crabby having been with her until the early hours of the morning when her husband, suffering a tummy bug, had come home from the nightshift and walked in on them. Crabby, no knight in shining armour, had legged it, leaving her to take his beating as well as her own. And it was reasonable to assume that Robbo Crabby's sudden recovery and return to work had been motivated by a very angry husband intent on revenge.

The day had begun cloudy and murky, but now the sky had cleared and the winter sun was hot through the windscreen. However, the brighter weather did nothing to lift Andy Lukeson's gloom.

He turned into the car park of the pub where he had arranged to meet Blair, recalling too late, as he got from the car, that Blair had been dry for the best part of a year after he'd collapsed and had had a liver scare. A pub had been the wrong place to arrange to meet him.

Never one for diplomacy, Alfie Blair's greeting was, 'You look like shit, Andy.'

'Then I look like I feel, Alfie.'

'Heard you're standing in for Jack Porter.'

'That's right.'

'Cantankerous sod, Porter. But a good copper. Told him a hundred times if once that eating battered cod and chips every day would do for him. I'll have a cup of coffee. There. Now you don't have to piss around trying to find out if I'm still dry.'

'Twelve months. Great credit due, Alfie.'

'Eleven months, two weeks, three days, twelve hours and,' he checked his watch, 'twenty-six minutes.' His smile was sad. 'Once the demon gets on your back he keeps riding you until you fall into the grave. And sometimes I wonder if it's worth the effort, Andy,' he confided, 'being miserable all the time.'

'In time it will ease.'

'Don't give me that shit,' he said crossly. 'Why are you here, anyway?'

'To talk about Sandra Fairweather.'

Blair groaned. 'Fairweather. The nail in the coffin of my promotion to Detective Chief Inspector.' The failure to catch Sandra Fairweather's killer probably had played a part in Alfie Blair being passed over for promotion, but more than likely it was his heavy drinking and irregular attendances which had been the main reason why he'd been overlooked. But there would be no getting him to admit that. Another DI and a DCI had also failed to bring Fairweather's killer to book, but it had been no consolation to Alfie Blair. No matter how many came after him, it had been his case and it had gone cold — the nightmare of every investigating officer, and right now Lukeson's also. 'Where did Fairweather pop up from again, Andy? Has something happened to bring her back to haunt us?'

'Nothing definite. You've heard about the murder in Loston, I take it?'

'Yeah. You've pulled it?'

'For my sins.'

'An Acting DI usually gets to make the tea and sandwiches, Andy. A stopper to push paper 'round until the real DI returns to duty. Porter must be done for,' he stated

165

bluntly. 'And you're obviously his replacement.'

'Jack Porter will die on the job, Alfie.'

Alfie Blair, several years older than Lukeson, studied him. 'You're shitting yourself, ain't you, son?' He took Lukeson's lack of reply as an answer. 'I know the feeling. On my maiden voyage, I couldn't see myself ever getting my man, woman as it turned out. I used to wake at night to the sound of laughter. All my erstwhile colleagues taking the piss when the case went cold on me.'

Lukeson appreciated the confidence.

'But the feeling of one-upmanship when I slapped cuffs on Helena Stafford for doing her old man in was special.' He chuckled. 'For all of three days I had to wear a larger shirt to accommodate my puffed up chest.'

He sipped the coffee the barman brought.

'So what is it you want to know about Sandra Fairweather, then?'

'I'm not sure.'

DI Alfie Blair laughed. 'Wrong answer, son. You're a DI now, so you're suppose to have all the answers. A Brigham girl. Found in Cobley Wood, the corner of the bloody place that's on Brigham's patch, worse luck. Strangled with the belt of her coat. Hadn't been fiddled with. Not a spot of trace evidence at the scene. Uphill right from the

166

start,' he said glumly. 'Are you good for a ploughman's?'

'Yes. Sorry.' Andy Lukeson ordered the ploughman's lunch. 'Not much to work with, Alfie,' he empathized. 'Did you have any suspects?'

'No.'

'None at all?'

'No one that looked a possible. There was an on and off boyfriend, and a bloke who lived in the flat above Fairweather who, according to her sister, made a bit of a nuisance of himself. The boyfriend was in lock-up for being drunk and disorderly on the afternoon Fairweather was topped. And the bloke upstairs was away visiting his auntie in Sussex.'

'An aunt?'

'Before you start thinking that auntie told porkies to get her nephew out of the shit, she's a nun, and there were three other sisters present in the convent garden when they were strolling.'

'Anything about the body then?'

'Such as?'

'I don't know. I'm fishing.'

'She might as well have been topped by a ghost.'

'And the crime scene?'

'Forensics said they'd never examined a

crime scene that was so clean.'

'Which means the killer was very careful, or very lucky.'

'Or very knowledgeable?' Alfie Blair pondered.

'Meaning?'

'The killer might have known his forensics,' he said.

'A copper?'

Blair shrugged. 'Must admit that I thought about it at the time, Andy.'

'And?'

'Still thinking about it now. Could also be someone who was connected rather than active. A lab technician, maybe. Something like that. What about your crime scene?'

'Same.'

'So you're thinking, same killer?'

'Right now, hanging by my fingernails, I'm prepared to grasp at any straw,' Lukeson admitted honestly.

'The on and off boyfriend did kick up a rumpus about an engraved gold bracelet he'd given her. Accused us of nicking it.'

'A bracelet,' Lukeson said thoughtfully, thinking about the earring that was missing from the murdered woman in Loston. 'There was an earring missing from the woman in Loston.'

'Trophies?' Blair pondered.

'Could be. Fairweather and she were not far apart in age. And both women were strangled.'

'Popular, strangulation.'

'Enjoy your lunch, Alfie,' Lukeson said.

'Good luck. Hope your career won't go belly up like mine did, Andy.'

'We both hope.'

'Keep me posted.'

'Thanks for your time, Alfie. If you think of anything else . . . '

'Yeah. Good ploughman's. Better still with a beer though. Don't worry,' Blair said, when Andy Lukeson glanced sharply at him. 'Being dry is hell. But being a soak is a bigger hell, Andy.'

Before driving away, he put in a call to Helen Rochester to have her check on cold cases of murdered women from whom some item had been taken. 'Fairweather had a bracelet taken. The woman in Layman's Park had a missing earring. So to begin with, search for women who had items of jewellery missing, Helen.'

★ ★ ★

As usual, the station canteen smelled of hot cooking oil. However, it being Thursday it also smelled of curry, because on Thursdays chef (a grandiose title for a cook, and a mediocre one at that) dished up his Eastern Delights Specials, the actuality bearing nothing of the promise of the title. Individually, Andy Lukeson hated both smells but, combined, found them overpoweringly gut-wrenching.

Glancing as he passed by, he could see how downmarket the British diet had become, the unhealthy future which the fare was storing up for its citizens, and the whopping great cost it would impose on future generations to deal with its after-effects. The odd diner had the 'healthy option', an unappetizing ham and egg salad or alternatively cheese and ham, with limp lettuce and a handful of peppers and corn which apparently did not want to insult the lettuce by appearing too fresh. A WPC had once been overheard to remark that the diet was responsible for the lack of 'sexual bottle' in her male colleagues. She had further opined that the canteen food was probably a senior officers' anti-copulation device to prevent any hanky-panky that might lead to questions being asked. Though not given to conspiracy theories, Andy Lukeson reckoned that the outspoken WPC might have been closer to the truth than she had imagined.

At least it was an explanation of sorts.

He spotted Sally Speckle at the far side of the busy canteen, gazing, preoccupied, out on the station car park, a depressing expanse of ancient tarmacadam that was, by the day if not the hour, being reclaimed by nature. Weeds poked through myriad cracks, and flourished uninhibitedly in the many pot-holes. Persistently pruned budgets had sidelined time and again the many promises to resurface the car park to prevent the ever increasing motoring costs of its users, and the probability of serious injury sooner or later. A couple of months previously when a PC, sprinting from a shower, had damaged an ankle in a water-filled pothole, there followed a flurry of promises to repair the surface, but again the tight-fisted mandarins who doled out police budgets came into play and the resurfacing of the car park had faded further and further into the distance, leaving the only hope now that a villain, being escorted indoors from the car park, fell foul of its uncertain underfoot conditions and kicked up a stink. Villains had rights, more than most, it seemed to honest law-abiding citizens.

'A penny for them,' Lukeson said, sitting at Speckle's table, belatedly thinking that he might not be welcome. 'Mind?'

'No, Andy. Not at all.'

She did not sound convincing.

'Can't be the breathtaking view that's taken you over,' he joked. Then: 'Look, it's pretty obvious you want to be alone, so I'll shove off.'

'Don't be daft,' she protested. 'A bit whacked. Didn't sleep very well. Think I might be coming down with something.' Like a lovebug, she thought.

The re-entry into her life of Simon Ambrose had opened a Pandora's box of emotions which she thought had been truly consigned to history, but the past had suddenly become the present and possibly the future also.

Simon had only been back in her life for a week (which had been intended to be only one night) and she was not at all sure that she wanted him out of it again, hence the one night which had turned in to a week. Of course, her feelings could simply be the stirrings of nostalgia, but could simple nostalgia have swept away the hurt and disappointment of Simon Ambrose's past betrayal and once again revived the possibility of a renewed relationship with him? She would have thought not. But human emotions were about as predictable as the direction of straw in a gale.

Disturbingly, he had not changed (except in shape and size, a few extra pounds round the waist and a few deep lines round his mouth and eyes, but he was ten years older), he was still charming, still had his impish humour and, in a more mature way, he was still as devastatingly attractive — at least to her he was. And that in a strange way disappointed and angered her, because she had always envisaged that were their paths to cross again post-betrayal, she would freeze him out with a look or a cutting word or two. But that had not happened, and she felt that she had let herself down.

Gone was the madcap and impetuous Simon, to be replaced by a more considerate man, much more to her liking. He had aged gracefully. He was, she considered, just about right for thirty-two years old. The startling good looks of the younger Simon had given way to an alluring maturity of jawline; his hair had thinned and receded a little, and surprisingly had become more unruly for one who had always been tonsorially well groomed. He needed a haircut badly, but she had not yet felt comfortable enough to suggest as much. His eyes were different; still brown and smoky and utterly riveting, but also touched with a sadness — no, a forlornness, which she hoped she would find the courage to ask him about.

The evening before, she had reached out

for milk and their hands had touched and the effect had been electric, just as it had been all those years ago. There had been a second when they might have . . . She had convinced herself that it was she who had pulled back from the brink, but she wasn't at all sure that it was not Simon who had retreated. It was an incident that had kept her awake most of the night and had haunted her a thousand times since. What if? She couldn't help wonder.

She sensed Andy Lukeson's curious scrutiny.

'How's the investigation coming along?' she enquired which, with her introspective mood, was as much interest as she could manage.

'It isn't,' he said gloomily. 'Thought I had a live suspect, but he's got an alibi.'

'Early days, Andy.' Sally Speckle's lopsided smile was one that always got deep inside Lukeson and gave him a warm glow. 'You're haunted by the fear that you're going to cock it up, aren't you?' she observed shrewdly. He thought about an outright and spirited denial, but ended simply hunching his shoulders like a schoolboy who had pretended to have the answer but had had his bluff called. 'Of all in Loston CID, Andy, you're the least likely to have a cold case on your hands.'

'You sound convinced,' he said. 'Pity I'm not as certain, Sally. Right now I think the gods have turned against me.'

There was that lop-sided smile again.

He had joined Speckle to pick her brains, but at that moment it was the last thing he wanted to do. His every instinct was to enquire about her male guest and the change he had seemed to have made in Sally Speckle's life — common gossip round the station. She even looked different, more at ease in herself. She had, or so it seemed to him, a new zest about her, like one might have at the start of a love affair.

'The gods have turned against you, Andy?'

'A second related murder. Well, as it stands of this moment, an attempted murder, which will soon become murder. This woman claimed she knew the killer but, unfortunately, she lapsed into a coma before she got round to telling me who it is.'

'Knew the killer?'

'Yes. She saw a man following the woman into Layman's Park. The silly thing about all of this is that Bridie Murphy reckoned that she could squeeze a couple of quid out of him before she phoned me. But he popped round and hit her with something heavy and blunt.'

'Blackmail,' Speckle said, her sympathy for Bridie Murphy clearly diminished.

'Blackmail, I reckon is a bit strong a description for what she had in mind,'

175

Lukeson defended Murphy.

'A dangerous game to play, Andy. As she obviously learned.'

'Easy to be critical when you've got three square meals a day and a nice bed to sleep in, alone, if that's what you want,' he said pointedly.

'This woman,' Speckle said, breaking a tense silence. 'You seem very sympathetic to her?'

'You'd like to know what a worn out, much abused prostitute meant to me, right?'

'Sorry, it's really none of my business.'

'Bridie Murphy, I believe, under more favourable circumstances could have been anything she'd wanted to be. But she was one of life's victims, Sally. Orphanage at six years old, half starved and physically abused. She once told me that there had hardly been a day in which she had not been beaten. No education, and on a boat to England at sixteen. Picked up by a pimp at Paddington when she got off the boat train. What chance did she have.

'One bitterly cold and snowy night when I was on the beat, I first came across Bridie. A bloke who's idea of a night out was to beat a woman unconscious was laying into her in a laneway. The more experienced officer with me said that I should keep walking. I didn't

176

agree, so I intervened.'

'How was the woman in the park killed, Andy?'

'Strangled.'

'Manual?'

Lukeson shook his head. 'Probably a scarf. A woollen scarf. There was a yellow wool thread snagged on a bush.'

'A wool scarf?' Speckle enquired quietly.

'Yes. A yellow wool scarf, if the snagged thread is an indicator.'

'Yellow?'

'Yes.'

Sally Speckle's mind was full of the yellow wool scarf Simon Ambrose had been wearing when she had met him, a scarf that she could not recall him having worn recently. She was unable to fix when she had last seen him wearing it. And he had been a bit withdrawn. A couple of times when she had spoken to him, he'd seemed to be in a world of his own. But what was she thinking, Simon Ambrose was no murderer!

'Must be lots of yellow scarves in Loston, Andy.'

Andy Lukeson wondered about Speckle's sudden edginess.

'Bridie Murphy witnessed a disagreement between two men outside the Coachman's Inn, where the murdered woman had gone with a man. The argument had spilled over from the pub. This other man had tried to move in when the man who was with the woman went to the loo.

'Later, when she pitched both men to blazes and went her own way and the men went back inside, Bridie Murphy said she saw a yellow scarf on the ground outside the pub. One of the men had been wearing a yellow scarf.'

'And you think the man who followed her into Layman's Park retrieved the scarf and used it as the murder weapon?' Speckle asked.

'That could be the way of things. But it could also be that the man who had been wearing it followed her.'

'But he went back inside, didn't he?'

'Yes. But he could have popped back out. Both men would have a motive. Rejection. Anger. Lust. Powerful reasons to murder.'

'CCTV?'

'The Coachman's Inn has only one CCTV camera,' Lukeson said. 'And that's to watch for sticky fingers at the cash register.'

'A pub without CCTV is a bit unusual.'

'The clientele of the Coachman's Inn are a shy lot. Mostly villains, prostitutes and punters. Don't care much for cameras.'

'The street, then?'

'Nothing worth having CCTV for. Mostly derelict buildings. Nothing worth nicking.'

'Layman's Park is home to all sorts of nasties at night,' Speckle said. 'A bit silly of this woman to be there.'

Speckle's comment surprised Lukeson, because it was completely out of character. Sally Speckle was a considerate woman, not given to the kind of bitter criticism she had just mouthed. 'That didn't give anyone a licence to murder her, Sally,' he said sharply. 'If everyone who did something silly was — '

'Don't get on my back, Andy,' Speckle interjected. 'Any reason why she should have gone into the park?'

'Possibly a short cut home.'

'She lives near the park then?'

'Not established. The short cut idea is just that, an idea. But her killer was not a down and out or an addict.'

'That's very positive. How can you be so certain?'

'Because I doubt very much if they'd have waited to sweep the ground at the crime scene.'

'Sweep the ground? What're you saying, the killer came with a sweeping brush? That's a first, Andy.'

'The crime scene is a place called Bonkers' Copse. It's more or less a circle of overgrown bushes and vegetation, the centre of which, getting very little chance to dry out, consists of soft, damp soil. Very good for footprints.

'To the front of the copse there's a newly laid cement path with a fully functioning light. To the rear of the copse, the reverse applies. Rough underlay for a new path waiting to be laid, and a vandalized light.

'So the killer had a choice of escape routes: a well lit new concrete path which would leave nice clear muddy footprints, or a rough path that would leave no impressions and total darkness. But that would still leave the soft soil in the copse. There was a sapling to the rear of the copse with a branch broken off. The soil looked as if it had been raked. I think the killer used the branch of the sapling to brush away his footprints as he retreated.'

'A murderer of the calm, cool and collected school of killers,' Speckle said. 'If the killer is of that breed, he'll be hard to catch, Andy.'

'A right old merry-go-round, isn't it?' Lukeson groaned.

'Every murder is, until the merry-go-round stops and there's only one left on it.'

Lukeson sat wearily back in his chair. Looking at the sparrow's meal on Speckle's plate, which she had ignored, he said, 'You're right off your grub, aren't you.'

'Just nibbling. Saving myself for later. Dinner.'

'Oh?' Lukeson tried to sound neutral and disinterested, but only managed to sound all the more curious. 'Where?'

Speckle shot him a look that said: any of your business? But said, 'Lorenzo's.'

'La-di-da. Won Lotto, have you?'

'With a friend, Andy.'

'Just popped over on the yacht from Monaco, has he?' he said, keeping a tight rein on his jealousy, but not quite succeeding to mask it completely.

'An old friend from my Uni days.'

She had not denied that the friend was male.

'Ah, a professor, then. Lots of Uni talk.'

'Or graddie chat, one might say,' she said, using the derogatory term used by traditional officers for graduates who had joined the police through the Graduate Recruitment Programme.

Andy Lukeson kicked himself. He had gone too far, and had not done himself any favours. Why shouldn't Sally Speckle have dinner with a friend? It was none of his bloody affair, was it?

Was it?

'Ah! Heads together time! *Acting* DI Lukeson looking for advice, Inspector?'

181

It was not often Andy Lukeson welcomed the presence or intervention of senior officers, but right then, despite the note of derision in her voice, he could have kissed ACC Alice Mulgrave. However, kissing Frank 'Sermon' Doyle would be a step too far, even for England.

'Hardly ma'am,' Sally Speckle said. '*DI* Lukeson is, in my opinion, one of the sharpest minds round here. The advice giver rather than the advice seeker, you might say.'

Doyle asked, 'Any progress on the Layman's Park matter, Lukeson?' Lukeson hunched his shoulders. The gesture of evasiveness did not please Doyle. 'Any possible suspects raising their heads above the parapet?'

'I'm hopeful, sir, that a swift conclusion will be reached,' Lukeson replied neutrally, not wanting the bother of having to run through all he had already gone over with Speckle.

It was a non-answer, but Doyle, conscious of wading into dangerous waters in the presence of a senior officer, chose not to press Lukeson. But the Chief Super made a point of letting the look he cast Lukeson speak louder than a thousand words. At some point along the line, Andy Lukeson knew that Doyle would have the skin off his back. But that was for another day. And right now he had more than enough on his plate to be going on with. Fortunately, it did not appear that Doyle or Mulgrave had heard about the assault on Bridie Murphy and its link to the woman in the park. And he was not about to tell them.

'How's the chicken pie?' Doyle asked, ready to accept an answer from either Speckle or Lukeson, and, getting one from neither, 'Some days it can be quite tasty,' he told Mulgrave.

'I detest chicken, Superintendent,' Mulgrave said. Doyle's face was a picture. 'And chicken pie is even more detestable.' She grimaced. 'All those unidentified bits.'

'Doesn't suit everyone, of course, ma'am,' Doyle said. 'I'll expect a prelim report on my desk post haste, Lukeson,' he said briskly. 'And a quick end to this affair would be appreciated.'

'Yes, sir,' Lukeson said compliantly. 'I'll do my best.'

'Good,' Mulgrave said, in her clipped military fashion. Although she had only been a very short time in her role, the appellation of 'Ballbuster', which DC Charlie Johnson had ascribed to Alice Mulgrave, seemed appropriate. 'I'm sure the Chief Constable, with whom I'll be meeting later this evening, will be keen to keep in touch with developments in a case that could so easily become . . . difficult, an embarrassment,' she settled her gaze on Andy Lukeson, 'were the investigation to bog down.'

She walked on, Doyle a suitable distance behind (some might say a lackey's distance behind, Andy Lukeson thought) glaring back at Lukeson, then switching to Speckle, letting both of them know in no uncertain manner that he had not appreciated their double act.

'If I can help in any way,' Sally Speckle told a downcast Andy Lukeson.

'Thanks.'

'You'll catch him, Andy,' she said brightly, a great deal brighter than she was feeling with the dark thoughts running through her mind.

Lukeson's sigh was world weary. 'I wish I had as much confidence in me as you seem to have, Sally. Mel Burnett, the mother of the child who found the body, had an idea that she had seen the dead woman before. Possibly in the redlight district, where Burnett worked in a newsagent's shop. Thought she might have come into the shop. But if she did see her there, I doubt very much if it was as a prostitute.'

'Why?'

'Instinct mainly.'

'A lot of prostitutes, when dolled up, can

look like princesses, Andy.'

'Maybe. But if she had been on the game, what was she doing in a grotty public park, and an even grottier part of it? A bit unusual nowadays to even take a scrubber to the park. It's akin to back against the wall in an alley. Things have moved on, even at the lower end of the market, Sally.'

'Get a couple of PCs to flash her photograph around the redlight district. If there's been dirty work afoot with one of their own, they'll be eager to cooperate. It could always be someone else's turn next.

'The punter may have liked the setting. Grottiness, for some, can be a turn on, Andy. And, being a Friday night, it's not beyond belief that some bloke might have stumbled out of a boozer and fancy something more than a chicken supper.'

Andy Lukeson said morosely, 'Speaking of chicken suppers. Seeing that I'm not dining out tonight, I'd better see what's on offer here.'

'Sarge!' Lukeson spun round on hearing Helen Rochester's summons.

'That'll be Inspector, girl,' a DS sitting at a nearby table intoned in a panto villain's voice.

'Shut your gob, Deasy!' Lukeson commanded. 'What is it, Helen?'

'Just something that came up when I was

chatting with PC Alan Walsh.' He was rumoured to be the new male interest in Helen Rochester's life. 'A complaint about a stalker, made by a woman called Anne Smith with an address in Roysneath Grove. That's just a street away from Layman's Park, and in the right direction for someone who might take a short cut across the park. Interesting, eh? She thinks that it's the same man who had bothered her in Birmingham, where she previously lived before moving here a couple of months ago.'

'Birmingham is a long way to come just to make a nuisance of himself.'

'It was a bit more than that. She claims that this man garrotted her cat with a piece of electric flex and stuffed its dead body through her letter box with a note attached, telling her that he'd do the same to her if he ever saw her with another man. And this was on a morning after a night out with a male friend.'

'When was this?'

'A year ago.'

'A year is a long time to wait if, as it seems, her stalker was obsessed with her. Was this man arrested?'

'No. She didn't make a complaint at the time.'

'Why not?'

'Afraid.'

'That's bloody silly.'

'But understandable,' Rochester said.

'If she had made a complaint, this man would have been questioned and possibly charged.'

'People . . . *women*, hope that these things will go away, Andy.'

'Well they seldom do.'

'Going to court is a heck of a gamble. Sometimes it's simply easier to forget and hope. Smith had no real evidence to offer. Contact was by phone.'

'Phone?' Lukeson groaned. 'You mean that's all this man was, a voice on the phone? So how did she know he was stalking her?'

'He'd mention things, like what she was wearing that day, places she had gone, the time she got home. Where she'd been the night before.'

'Is he phoning her now?'

'No. She has an unlisted number. But she believes that he pops in most days to where she works. Anne Smith works for a wholesale electrical supplier. The man comes in almost every day. She believes it's the same voice that she heard on the phone.'

'That's a bit thin. Phones change voices,' Lukeson said. 'Not many people sound the same in person as they do on the phone.'

'Her cat was garrotted with electric flex

and this man is obviously an electrician, or at least something to do with the electrical trade. And what really prompted her to report all of this was when, a couple of days before he turned up at her place of work, she saw him in a pub — '

'The Coachman's Inn?' Lukeson enquired hopefully.

'No. But a pub not far away. The Unicorn. Just round the corner, you might say. When he saw Smith, he took a length of electric flex from his pocket and toyed with it. She took that as a message to her. Now, the woman in Layman's Park was strangled. Not with electric flex, but maybe he uses what's to hand.'

'A big leap from garrotting a cat to strangling a woman,' Lukeson said.

Rochester pointed out: 'A lot of serial killers liked to practice on animals.'

'His name?' Lukeson enquired.

Rochester shook her head. 'Never signs anything. Doesn't use a credit card. Pays cash. And it seems he needs to be close to her, because sometimes he buys something small, like a pack of light bulbs which he could pick up in any supermarket.'

'Have the wholesalers watched,' Lukeson said decisively. 'When he turns up next time, have Ms Smith come to a window or follow him outside discreetly. We'll have a word. Perhaps, as he's given us all this information, PC Walsh might like to follow through, eh?'

'Yeah. I'm sure he would, Andy,' Rochester said, obviously chuffed.

Sally Speckle's mobile rang. 'Oh, Simon . . . '

Was it his imagination, or had Speckle's edginess increased? If it was edginess, then it was something new to her and to Lukeson. 'The man with oceans of dosh, I reckon,' he said in a whispered aside to Rochester. 'Off to din-dins at Lorenzo's tonight.' There was no mistaking the bitter under-current in Andy Lukeson's gossipy confidence.

Was Lukeson jealous?

'Do I?' Speckle said. 'No. I'm not feeling down.'

'Come on, then.' Lukeson sprang off his chair. 'No time to be standing round twiddling our thumbs, Sergeant!'

'Sir,' Helen Rochester said, playing catch-up as Lukeson strode ahead.

'Message for you, sir.' A wet behind the ears WPC bravely blocked Lukeson's path. 'Two, actually,' she said as an afterthought, not in the least as assured in dealing with a senior rank as she would have one believe.

'Popular fellow, aren't I, WPC Rafter,' Lukeson teased.

Rafter was at a loss as to how to respond;

189

to agree would sound condescending, and to not agree might be an affront.

'DI Lukeson hasn't taken his bowl of bran today, Cilla,' Rochester said. A remark which seemed to completely unnerve the young WPC. 'The messages,' she coaxed.

'Oh, yeah,' Cilla Rafter's hand fluttered with her bobbed blond hair, of which there wasn't enough of, to flutter with. 'The first was from Brigham. DI Blair . . . '

'Oh, yes,' Lukeson encouraged.

'DI Blair said to tell you that there was one peculiar aspect to the Fairweather murder.' Her brow furrowed. 'He said to tell you that that crime scene had been — '

'Swept?'

'Yes, sir,' Rafter said, still not sure that she had got Blair's message correctly. 'Makes sense, does it, sir,' she checked.

'I think it does indeed, WPC Rafter,' Lukeson said. 'And the second message?'

'That was from a Ms Burnett. She said that her little girl remembered where she had seen the woman in Layman's Park before.'

'I am having a good day,' Lukeson said.

'She says that it was at the shopping centre near her. She, the woman, was handing out leaflets drumming up business for an insurance company.'

'Did she say which one?'

'She couldn't recall, sir. But she says that it's the one on telly with the dancing polar bear. And that would be Top Hat Insurance, sir.' WPC Rafter giggled. 'That polar bear makes me laugh every time I see him in top hat and tails, doing that silly dance.'

'It's only silly because the bear is not Fred Astaire. He danced it magically.'

'Fred Astaire? Another bear, is he, sir?'

'WPC Rafter,' Lukeson enthused. 'You are an absolute angel who one day, I have no doubt, will become Chief Constable.'

'Crikey! You reckon, sir.'

'Oh, I do, Rafter. I most assuredly do.'

'Oh, dear.' WPC Rafter's hand fluttered at her hair again, and there was a distinct colouring of her already rosy cheeks.

'OK, then,' Lukeson said to Rochester. 'Where to next, eh?'

'Top Hat Insurance?'

'So much brainpower in the females round here,' he sighed. 'It's really staggering.'

'Shut it, Andy!' Rochester said.

WPC Cilla Rafter looked aghast at Rochester. Then she looked anxiously at Lukeson, obviously expecting fireworks, and clearly wishing that she was anywhere else — anywhere at all.

★ ★ ★

191

'That'll be our Mr Hampton,' said the receptionist at Top Hat Insurance when Andy Lukeson asked to speak with someone who might be able to help him with a staff matter.

'And your Mr Hampton is?' he enquired of the receptionist.

'HR,' she said briskly. Andy Lukeson reckoned that she would do everything briskly. 'It would help if I could tell him what this is about.'

'It's a police inquiry,' Lukeson replied a touch curtly, responding in kind to the receptionist's offhanded approach, dealing with him while at the same time doing several other things, the consummate multitasker, a breed who got up Andy Lukeson's nose. 'I think that's enough to be going on with?'

'If you'll take a seat,' she said, pointing to chairs at the far side of a very plush foyer, bringing the thought to mind that there was a lot of dosh in the insurance game, despite insurers' constant whining. 'I'll summon our Mr Hampton.'

And, summoned, Hampton would come running, he thought. Irrespective of his rank within Top Hat. The receptionist would be ignored at one's peril.

'Must be lots of dosh in the insurance game,' Helen Rochester observed, echoing Lukeson's thoughts, casting her eyes about

192

on their way to the plush chairs adjacent to a water fountain. 'I wonder if I tossed in a coin would I have a wish?'

'And what would you wish for?'

'A diet that works,' she said, deadpan.

'Is there one? Isn't it all down to willpower?'

'Willpower only works if you've got it, Andy. And if you have it, then you don't have a problem, do you. Because you'll have willpower.'

'A vicious circle,' he said, dropping into a chair. 'Maybe the dancing bear will pop in to entertain us while we wait.'

'Or maybe he'll be a real nasty bear who devours grumpy DIs.'

Ten minutes later, nine of which Andy Lukeson considered to be a waste of time, *our* Mr Hampton, portly, almost completely bald and with furtive eyes, entered the foyer from a door to the left of where Lukeson and Rochester were seated. 'Reginald Hampton,' he called out, soft pudgy, hand extended, the insurance salesman in him coming immediately to the fore on seeing other humans who just might, even though they were police officers, be potential customers.

'Looks more like a Working Men's Club comedian,' Rochester murmured.

Reginald Hampton's suit was expertly and

expensively tailored to camouflage his portliness, but it was a wasted expense, as an expanding girth ruined the length of the trousers by pulling them up short to reveal fawn socks with a black and amber box pattern, completely at odds with the quiet grey of his suit. Brown shoes did not help either.

Lukeson took his hand and hated its soft, damp feel. 'DI Lukeson and DS Rochester.'

Hampton looked to Rochester, who was wearing her official police smile, and Andy Lukeson could not decide which was worse, a professional insurance or a professional police grin. In any case, there wasn't much between them on the silly smiles scale.

'Now, then, in what way can Top Hat Insurance be of assistance to the constabulary?' By his cheeky chappy delivery, Hampton obviously thought he had said something to be laughed at. Neither Lukeson or Rochester followed his lead, and Hampton was left floundering between ignoring what was obviously a gaffe of sorts, and an attempt at humour which had sunk without trace.

Lukeson produced a photo of the dead woman, which sent Hampton into immediate shock. 'That's our Ms Blake!' His jaw dropped. 'She looks . . . oh, dear.'

'Is there somewhere more private we can

talk, sir?' Lukeson enquired.

'Yes. Would you arrange for coffee to be sent to my office, Ms Archer,' he called to reception.

'Right away, Mr Hampton,' Ms Archer responded, briskly, of course, while loading a computer printer with paper.

Hampton led the way to the lift. 'An accident, was it?'

'No,' Lukeson replied.

Lukeson noted the tremor in Reginald Hampton's hand as he pressed the button to take them to floor three. 'It isn't . . . ? It can't be . . . '

The lift glided smoothly and silently upwards.

'Can't be, Mr Hampton?' Lukeson prompted.

'Well.' He fidgeted with his watch. 'This woman in . . . but it can't be, surely. Kate was such an inoffensive woman.' Both Lukeson and Rochester noted the familiar use of Blake's first name. 'It isn't, is it? I mean the woman in Layman's Park?'

The lift stopped climbing and the doors slid open.

'Regrettably, it would seem so, Mr Hampton,' Lukeson said.

'Was she mur-murdered?'

'Ms Blake was a popular colleague, was she?' Lukeson enquired.

'Oh, yes,' he said enthusiastically. 'Kate was . . . '

'Was?' Lukeson prompted.

'Very well liked.' Helen Rochester thought: Especially by you, eh, Reggie. 'A thug looking for easy pickings I suppose?'

'All possibilities are, of course, being considered, sir,' Andy Lukeson said diplomatically.

'It had to be someone deranged,' Hampton said, as they progressed along the hall from the lift to his office. 'One thinks of that type of person as belonging to London or someplace like that. But here in Loston.' He shook his head, his shiny baldness reflecting the strip lighting overhead, in a hallway that had none of the glitz of reception, being strictly functional and out of bounds to the public. 'That must be it. Poor Kate fell foul of some lunatic.'

Or perhaps a spurned suitor, Lukeson thought.

'We'll need Ms Blake's address.'

'Flat 6, 12 Cramer Street. Quite close to the park. Not the best area, is it. I urged Ka . . . Ms Blake,' he corrected, obviously conscious this time of the use of Blake's first name and the impression it might make on the police, Lukeson reckoned, 'to move to a better area.' Both Lukeson and Rochester noted the readiness with which Hampton was able to provide Kate Blake's address.

Reginald Hampton had either a total grasp of employee details or he knew Kate Blake's address for another reason. 'An attractive young woman, in a not so attractive area was always going to be problematic. What was she doing in that awful park late at night?' His question was directed at Andy Lukeson.

'Late at night, sir? I don't recall mentioning the time of Ms Blake's death.'

'Well, I assumed . . . '

Had he, as he said, assumed? Lukeson wondered. Or might Hampton have known that Kate Blake had been murdered late at night because he had killed her?

'Why she was in the park hasn't become clear yet,' Lukeson said. 'She might have been taking a short cut home. That's one theory. Know Layman's Park well, do you, sir?'

'Good God, no! A dreadful place. Hardly ever out of the newspapers, is it. That whole area.'

'Employ many people, do you?' Lukeson enquired conversationally.

'Here, you mean? In Loston?'

'Yes.'

'Almost three hundred, Inspector.'

'Indeed. That's quite a number.'

'Several thousand countrywide.'

'Did Ms Blake occupy an important position in the company?'

'Oh, no. Just a clerk. But a clerk with great potential.'

Rochester and Lukeson's eyes clashed, and it was obvious that their thoughts were as one. Almost three hundred employees and Hampton could reel off instantly the address of a single employee, who was a mere cog in the machine, and a small one at that. Two possibilities: either Hampton had an encyclopaedic knowledge of staff, or an exclusive knowledge of one member of staff.

Acting DI Lukeson wondered which. The latter, Rochester reckoned.

Hampton turned in through a door which announced his name in plastic letters of which the R in Reginald was lopsided. Lukeson looked about at other doors with plastic names, suggesting to Lukeson many changes. Whip one set of plastic letters off, and hey presto, the office became the immediate domain of the next occupant. He thought that it must give employees a nervousness which was probably designed to make them continuously look over their shoulder and consequently to labour harder.

Hampton went straight to his laptop, and Kate Blake's file flashed on screen.

'I'm sure you'll find anything you need in there, Inspector,' he said, turning the laptop towards him. 'Not that there's much personal stuff. She hadn't worked for us for very long. Mostly her CV and a recommendation by her upcoming section manager that she be considered for promotion.'

'Could I have a printout?'

'I'd have to check with Legal. There's a hundred and one ways now in which a company can fall foul, you understand. And that would never do.'

Not if you wanted your name to remain on the door, Lukeson reckoned.

'It's the age of rights, isn't it.'

'Could you check with your legal department then,' Rochester asked.

'Yes. Right away.' He picked up an extension phone and punched out a three-digit number. 'Hampton. Is Henry about?' He smiled at Lukeson and Rochester as he waited. 'Henry, old man. I have the police here with me. Oh, nothing like that.' Whatever *that* was. 'It's about Kate Blake. Oh, of course, you haven't heard. She was murdered. Yes, murdered. She was the woman found in Layman's Park. Naturally, the police are making inquiries, and they would like a printout of her HR file. Of course to take away with them,' Hampton said impatiently. He listened attentively, but less so as the voice on the phone droned on. 'Look, Henry,' Hampton snapped. 'I don't need bell, book and candle, old man. I see. And if they insist?' He rolled his eyes. 'Yes, Henry. I'll explain.' He listened again. 'No. Margery wants to visit her brother in Bournemouth the coming Saturday. Enjoy.'

He hung up.

'Golf,' he explained. 'Henry Ruskin is the passionate kind. Hail, rain or snow.'

'The printout?' Lukeson said.

'Yes. The printout.' Reginald Hampton's fleshy shoulders drooped. 'Legal can see all sorts of problems, I'm afraid. They always do. You'll have to go through channels, Inspector. Sorry.'

'We have a murder on our hands, Mr Hampton,' Andy Lukeson said in a clipped tone. 'Time is all-important. The killer is going further into the mist all the time.'

'I can appreciate that,' Hampton said. 'But being a police officer you must understand the kind of legal pit that might open up. It's our experience that we're fast catching up on America in our readiness to start litigation proceedings at the drop of a hat.'

'Would that be a top hat,' Lukeson intoned annoyedly.

'Perhaps if your superiors and my superiors got together the matter can be resolved quickly, Inspector,' Hampton said petulantly.

'I'm sure that Ms Blake's killer would like

that to happen. Any time we waste, he or she gains.'

'I'm sorry, Inspector. My hands are tied. That's as far as it goes for now. You must understand that employees of Top Hat Insurance are entitled to — '

'How well did you know Ms Blake?' Lukeson interrupted brusquely.

'Know her, Inspector?' Hampton asked vaguely, hedging until he thought through the question and any implications inherent in it.

'It's a simple enough question, Mr Hampton.' Lukeson's voice was laden with official frost. Hampton was rattled. Helen Rochester concentrated on reading Kate Blake's file on screen. Reginald Hampton squirmed. Andy Lukeson knew that he had opened the proverbial can of worms. 'It would be better if you cleared the air now, Mr Hampton,' he said confidently. Hampton squirmed even more. 'You are, as far as possible, guaranteed confidentiality, sir.'

He protested. 'Look, I can't see how you'd think — '

'You gave us Kate Blake's address without having to think, even though by your own admission she was a relatively minor employee, and one of three hundred.' Hampton's desperation was palpable. 'And you've referred to her continuously as Kate rather than the more formal Ms Blake.'

Hampton slumped in his desk chair.

'I dropped round to her flat once or twice,' he admitted.

'You were in a relationship with Ms Blake?'

'I wouldn't call it a relationship, Inspector. More of a silly episode. I'm really a very happily married man.' There was pleading in his eyes. 'This is terribly difficult.'

'So is murder, for the victim,' Lukeson said unsympathetically.

'It's company policy that there be no relationships between rank and file and management.' Lukeson remained impassive. 'Kate could be manipulative.'

'Meaning?'

'Pleasure for profit or for advancement?' Hampton said. 'Oh, not cash in hand, you understand. When I say profit, I mean salary enhancement by advancement.'

'You and she struck a bargain, eh?'

'If mention of promotion was made, I would not put any obstacles in her way. In fact, I would encourage and endorse her promotion. Though, frankly, I did not consider her to be suitable.'

Andy Lukeson's guess had been a shrewd one.

'I recall that in her file there was a recommendation by her upcoming section manager that she be promoted. Did you endorse it?'

'I hadn't got round to it. But it doesn't matter now, does it.'

'*Upcoming?*'

'Sorry?'

'Upcoming section manager,' Lukeson said.

'Oh, that. Yes. Upcoming means that the promotion had been agreed as soon as the present incumbent vacated the post.'

'And what is the name of this *upcoming* chap?'

'Nick Clark. Look, Inspector, if my ah . . . association with Ms Blake becomes common knowledge, I'm out on my ear. Here and at home.'

'It won't, if it's not relevant to bringing our killer to justice.' Hampton's relief was brief. 'Where were you on the 6th between 11 p.m. and 1 a.m. on the 7th?'

'In bed.'

'Alone?'

'At home. With my wife. I went to bed at 11.30, after some friends left.'

'We'll need your friends' names and addresses.'

'There's no need for that, surely. My wife will verify that I was with her. Anyway, you can't think that I had anything to do with

Kate Blake's murder?'

'How long have you and your wife been married, Mr Hampton?'

'Twenty-nine years. Why?'

'A long time. A wife might do or say anything to remain in a stable relationship. It wouldn't be easy to up roots after such a long time together.'

He snorted. 'You think my wife might lie for me?' Andy Lukeson's silence answered Hampton's question. 'My wife is a vicar's daughter. A lie, for her, would mean eternal damnation.' His tone of voice was tired, bored. Lukeson reckoned that if his wife was as upright as he had stated she was, Reginald Hampton had probably long since grown weary of living a life of righteousness in his wife's mission to avoid damnation and get hell over with on earth. 'Besides, if it's verification of my whereabouts between 11 p.m. and 1 a.m., my friends will be pretty useless, since they went home at 10.30 Inspector.'

'That is a point, sir,' Lukeson conceded.

Lukeson cast a glance at a framed photograph on Hampton's desk of a very happy young graduate, hugging Hampton and a woman, a little younger than Hampton but only by a year or two. The young man's likeness of feature to the woman left little doubt that she was his mother. 'A happy occasion?' he commented.

'Yes indeed,' Hampton agreed proudly. 'Charles is our only son, our only child. Well on the road to being a ground-breaking physicist, I'm told by those who know about these things.'

'Abroad, is he?'

'No. He's actually not that far away. London.'

'That's nice.'

'Yes. It would have broken his mother's heart had he to go further afield. But he really had the pick of posts,' he boasted.

Andy Lukeson smiled. 'His father's brains, no doubt.'

Hampton sighed. 'Alas not, Inspector. Following in his uncle Bertie's footsteps, my wife's brother. Frankly, I wasn't very good at maths in school or college. Algebra and graphs and that kind of thing actually bore me senseless.'

'Come home often, does he?' Lukeson enquired.

'As often as his hectic lifestyle permits. He's just returned to London this morning actually, after a few days off.'

'Spent with his adoring parents?'

'Hopefully, he thinks well of us, Inspector. He tries to visit as often as he can. A family man yourself?' Hampton enquired.

'A stodgy old bachelor, I'm afraid.'

'Well, it's said that police work and family happiness don't mix very well.'

'Indeed. Very fond of mummy, I'd say,' Lukeson said. 'May I?' he picked up the photograph on the desk.

'They're very close. Always have been. A mutual appreciation society, actually, which is almost nigh impossible to join,' he added, an edge of bitterness to his voice.

Wife a doting mother, instead of a loving wife? The reason for Hampton's dalliance with Kate Blake?

'Had one of those,' Lukeson said, indicating the flowing woollen scarf that the younger Hampton was wearing. 'Kept the neck muscles supple, I found.'

Not given to social chatter while on official business, up to that point Helen Rochester had been wondering about Lukeson's sudden loquaciousness, and now she understood — the scarf Hampton's son was wearing. It looked dark in colour, but he just might have, or have had, a yellow scarf. And having just returned to London that morning, mummy's boy was around at the time of Blake's murder.

'Wears the bloody things threadbare,' Hampton grunted. 'I don't think I've ever

206

seen him without one between September and May. Can't abide anything round my neck myself. Makes me feel as if I'm choking.'

Information gathered, Andy Lukeson put the photograph back on Hampton's desk.

'We're about done I think,' he said. Hampton's relief was obvious. 'If I need anything further, I'll get back to you, Mr Hampton. Oh, was your son at home when you had friends in?'

'No. Out somewhere.'

Reginald Hampton gave a little laugh. 'I'll see you off the premises, so to speak, Inspector.'

'Oh, that won't be necessary, sir. I'm sure my colleague will remember the way.' And, hopefully, any relevant details from Kate Blake's file which she had been perusing during his questioning of Hampton.

Hampton waited at his office door until they entered the lift, waving to them in a manner one might to a departing friend as they did so.

'And Hampton junior's motive is?' Helen Rochester said, as the doors of the lift slid soundlessly shut.

'Daddy playing around, hurting mummy. Can't top daddy, because that would also hurt mummy . . . '

'So remove daddy's bit on the side, and all

is hunky dory again?' Rochester said.

'Bingo!'

'It's a theory, Andy.'

'Indeed it is, Sergeant,' Lukeson responded, as the lift doors opened on the foyer.

Crossing the foyer, Lukeson wondered about what had happened to the coffee which Hampton had ordered? Ms Archer was still busy multitasking, much, much too busy to reply to Lukeson's goodbye.

12

'Are you sure you can afford this, Simon?' Sally Speckle checked, standing outside Lorenzo's, which occupied the ground floor of a very elegant and lovingly preserved Georgian house. 'How much did you win on that horse?'

'Enough,' Ambrose said, annoyedly waving aside her question.

'I feel guilty, Simon.'

'Guilty?' he scoffed. 'Why should you feel guilty?'

Sally Speckle's thoughts went back to her canteen conversation with Andy Lukeson, and its disturbing mention of a yellow scarf which had been used to strangle the woman in Layman's Park. She had managed to convince herself that Simon Ambrose could not possibly be involved, but she was honest enough to admit to herself, on reflection, that the ease with which she had done so was down to hope and nostalgia (always viewed through rose-tinted glasses) more than to her training as a police officer. The facts were that on the night of the murder he had come home in the early hours and had not mentioned where he had been. But that could be down to the simple fact that where he had been was none of her business. He was, after all, a guest and nothing more. Or at least that was the pretence she liked to hang on to, born of past hurt pride and present doubt. Had she been the objective police officer, she would have told Lukeson about Simon having a scarf as he described, and about his late return on the night in question and the fact that Simon's yellow scarf seemed to have disappeared. But to do so would have stirred up a hornet's nest. Lukeson would have been compelled to question Simon Ambrose about his whereabouts. The source of that trouble for him would have been her, and that would most definitely have ended all possibility of them ever being friends again, let alone lovers. However, by remaining silent, she had acted in a manner not befitting a police officer, and she had reached the conclusion that, having done so, the question of her continuing to masquerade as such would be a betrayal of her promise to herself to at all times put the law before her personal feelings or reservations. On the other hand, she could put a reasonable argument that Simon's yellow scarf (after all, she had pointed out, there had to be a lot of yellow scarves about) and his late return could simply be coincidence and, had she told Lukeson, Simon Ambrose would have a perfectly checkable story to remove any doubt. However, no matter how she jumbled argument and counterargument, the one irrefutable fact was that she had not told Andy Lukeson when, as a police officer and a good friend (whose career would effectively be over were he not to catch the killer), she should have.

'You're very pensive,' Ambrose said. 'Bad day at the office?' Speckle shrugged. Her unease became all the more pronounced when the conversation took a turn that might have been small talk, or more worryingly, a quest for insider information on Simon Ambrose's part. 'Involved in that murder in the park?'

'No.'

'No? Loston's ace detective not involved.'

'Is that sarcasm, Simon?'

'Surprise. The monkfish is nice.'

'I'm not the fishy type.'

'As I recall, Sally. As a matter of fact, I've been thinking a lot about the past.'

'Oh?'

'You and me.'

'Oh?'

He laughed. 'I think the needle's stuck. Back to safer ground, I think. We have two choices. Work. Or that great British fallback, weather.'

'Sorry, Simon. I'm not very good company tonight.'

'A bit of an understatement, that, Sally. So what are you up to at present? Workwise, I mean.'

'Simon, it would be completely improper of me to — '

'In that case,' he interrupted brusquely. 'The weather is supposed to be getting milder from tomorrow.'

'I'm sorry, Simon.'

'Don't be.'

'Arranging all this and wasting it on a damp squib.'

'Sally,' he reached across the table and took her hands in his. 'I've been thinking . . . '

Not now Simon! Please, not now.

' . . . That maybe it's time I moved on.' It was not at all what she had expected him to say. She had, in her stupid pride, assumed that he had been engaging in a preamble to suggesting that they get back together. 'I don't fancy becoming clutter. You seem to have found your niche as a police officer, and I wouldn't want to muck it all up for you.' Muck it up for her? Had he admitted in a roundabout way that he had done something that would be incompatible with him being the guest of a police officer? He held Speckle's gaze. 'Might have met her, you know. The woman who was murdered in the park. Got in to a bit of a rumpus over her in a pub called the Coachman's Inn, I suspect.'

'Rumpus?'

Sally Speckle's voice came back to her from a long way off.

'Tried to cut in on this other chap. It all got a bit nasty.'

'Where's your yellow scarf, Simon?'

He hunched his shoulders. 'Lost it. Or it was nicked.'

'When did you lose it? Or when was it nicked?'

'The night the woman was murdered.' He frowned thoughtfully. 'Oh, I see. The newspapers say she was strangled. With a scarf?'

'Can you recall when you last had the scarf, Simon?'

'Always the copper, eh.'

'When, Simon?'

'I think I had it when the rumpus adjourned to outside the Coachman's Inn. After that, assuming that the murdered woman is one and the same as the woman in the Coachman's Inn, let me see how good a copper I'd have made. I was in a nearby pub. Argued over her. Rejected. Blood up, I followed her. Rejected again, but I was having none of it. So I took my scarf, wrapped it round her neck and choked the life out of her. Pretty feasible from a copper's point of view, wouldn't you say, Inspector?'

'The other man?'

'Went back inside with me.'

'Might he have slipped back out?'

'I wasn't his keeper, Sally. I was pretty well pissed by then anyway, and on my way to being totally pissed.'

'Did the woman mention his name?'

'Called him Nick, I think.'

'It was 2.45 when you arrived back. That's quite a gap between closing time and the time you arrived home.'

'I wandered about, the way drunks do. To be frank, can't remember how I got back to your place.' He looked her straight in the eye. 'I didn't murder her, Sally.'

'Did you see anyone when you left the Coachman's Inn, Simon?'

'Anyone?'

'A woman. Middle-aged.'

'Which one of the three are you interested in?'

'Three?'

'Joke, Sally. I was pissed, remember. I was seeing three of everything.' Speckle was not in a laughing mood.

Andy Lukeson had told her that Bridie Murphy had witnessed the argument outside the Coachman's Inn. So it's likely that seeing Simon again so soon, she'd have recognized him going into the park. But she had summoned Andy to the hospital to tell him the man's name, so that meant that she actually knew the man who had followed the murdered woman into Layman's Park, and that ruled Simon out. He was new to Loston. She couldn't have known his name.

Sally Speckle's relief was quickly snuffed out by her next dark thought.

Simon had been drunk. Bridie Murphy, a prostitute. A natural alliance. Drunks talked a lot. Simon might have given Murphy his name and where he was staying. Or she might have followed him home. Made contact for the blackmail she had in mind. Or, sober and realizing the danger he was in, Simon had acted to protect himself. Murphy might have taken him back to her flat, so he'd have known where she lived.

'I haven't as yet had to resort to picking up middle-aged whores, Sally,' Ambrose said solemnly. And in response to Speckle's wide-eyed innocence. 'A woman. Middle-aged. Late at night. Hanging around outside a pub, in an area a spit away from the redlight district . . .

'Do you know what was the uppermost thought in my mind, Sally? The thought that kept me wandering round for hours. It was of coming home and making love to you, if you'd have me. I stood outside your bedroom door, a frightened little boy trying to muster up the courage to knock. Would you have taken me into your bed, if I had?' Speckle did not answer, because she did not have an answer to give. 'So I saved my blushes and went to bed. Now,' he waved his hand over the dinner table, 'let's leave all of this. It wasn't a good idea to begin with.'

★   ★   ★

Sitting down to read the preliminary forensics reports on Kate Blake's murder and the attempted murder of Bridie Murphy, which in all probability would shortly be upgraded to murder also, Acting DI Andy Lukeson had a weariness about him. Usually his head hit the pillow and he was asleep, but he had not slept well, had woken grumpy, and not much had improved since, even after three cups of canteen coffee. More and more, he was following the well-worn path of other bachelor officers, depending on canteen fare rather than going to the bother of cooking — the route to obesity, Alec Balson had warned, and all its associated health problems. 'I could eat a horse and not put on an ounce,' had been Lukeson's response only six months before, but he was now giving the bathroom scales a wide berth. He had not, in appearance, put on weight, but he now avoided the stairs, preferring the lift, and the jeans he used to slum in on a day off no longer fitted as comfortably as they used to.

He browsed through the reports, which contained little of interest and even less of a useful nature. The reports were what investigating officers called 'quietners', served up to gain time when nothing significant had been found, filled with lots of theory, ifs and maybes, most of which would amount to nothing in the final report. Both scenes were described as challenging, a forensics euphemism for a total mess needing time to sort out, a *don't call us, we'll call you* message. He could complain, but to no effect. Forensics were used to complaints, and were well versed in saying a lot without giving any answers before their findings were conclusive and provable, always with an eye to the possible court proceedings ahead where their work would be dissected and rubbished by defence counsel if given the slightest chance. In fact, it was DI Jack Porter that Lukeson had heard to say that forensic officers were more politicians than the crowd of wankers in Parliament.

Blake's flat had been searched but nothing immediately relative to her murder had been found. There was, of course, trace evidence in the flat, but finding who it belonged to would be a long trawl through friends, visitors, relatives and whoever to eliminate them. But he could always hope that somewhere along the line that all-important titbit of DNA or a fingerprint would be discovered which would point him in the right direction. Police officers, particularly those with little to go on (he dreamed of DNA and fingerprints) had to be optimists.

He needed, as Balson had said, a rub of the green and quickly. Doyle would be back, looking for answers, and he had none to give. Frank 'Sermon' Doyle (normally a man of few words who had earned his nickname because of his long-windedness when it came to such things as the overtime budget) was a fair and considerate man, but that did not mean that, were he to believe that the officer leading an investigation was not up to the task, he would not hesitate to replace him or her. And, as in any other occupation, the stigma of being found wanting was difficult to overcome and in many cases impossible to remove.

Passing, Sally Speckle popped her head in the door.

'Good grief,' Lukeson said, yawning. 'You look almost as knackered as me. Coffee and a sticky bun. My treat.'

'Coffee, yes. Sticky bun, no. Not with what it costs to go to the dentist these days. Better check in first, though. Give me five minutes, Andy.'

Speckle went along the corridor to her office. She had spent a night of torment, caught between past loyalty and present duty. Arriving in the car park, her dilemma seemed to have resolved itself — she would tell Andy Lukeson about Simon Ambrose. Her resolve, which at that point had seemed unbreakable, had slowly slipped away between the car park and the moment she had popped her head in Lukeson's door. But she had already delayed too long. Taking courage, she spun round and made a determined dash along the hall to Lukeson's office, keeping her mind clear of all thoughts but one — to do her duty as a police officer. Were she to change her mind again, she would walk out of the building and, not considering herself worthy of the trust placed in her, she would not return again. But as an ordinary citizen, she would still be left with the duty to help the police with their inquiries, and a duty to one dead woman and another likely dead woman to unmask their killer.

'Ma'am . . .'

Would nothing go right! What could Anne Fenning want that couldn't wait? She turned into Lukeson's office, calling back, 'Later, Anne.'

'Can't wait.'

She was in the open door of Lukeson's office and about to say 'It will bloody have to!' when Fenning caught her up.

'Cecily Lamplin's been killed.'

13

'Killed?' Speckle queried, her emotions mixed, part regret that Cecily Lamplin was dead, and part relief that it could not have been Simon Ambrose who had killed her (not that she could see any reason why he would have unless, of course, he was a raving lunatic), because when she had left home thirty minutes before he was out for the count, having consumed enough alcohol when they had got back from their disastrous visit to Lorenzo's to keep him under for most of the day, and unfit to function for the remainder.

'Not murdered,' Fenning said, gauging perfectly the sum of Speckle's fears. 'Traffic accident. Knocked down at home by her husband.'

'Lamplin, did you say?' Andy Lukeson queried. 'Of Lamplin gardening fame?'

'Yes,' Fenning confirmed, Sally Speckle already on her way. 'Met him once at the Orchid Festival. Orchids are Lamplin's claim to fame. Didn't like him much.'

'Why not?'

'Felt he got in my knickers with one look.

Anyway, I don't fancy baldies. Should have some of the hair on his eyebrows transplanted to his head, if you ask me.'

'Thought you preferred the more mature man?'

'I do. But not the creepy kind.'

'Cecily Lamplin. Lamplin's wife?'

'Yeah.'

'The news seems to have knocked Sally for six,' Lukeson observed.

'The guv'nor's been involved. A burglary. The guv'nor had her doubts. The pieces didn't fit.' Fenning frowned. 'Died a death after the boss had a private chat with Rupert Lamplin, though. Charlie Johnson was none too pleased. Said it made him look like a chump. He responded to the original complaint, you see. When they left the Lamplin house, Charlie asked what her private chinwag with Lamplin was all about. Charlie says that the guv'nor asked if he trusted her. He said, of course, ma'am. And that was the end of that.'

That, Lukeson thought, was uncharacteristic behaviour for Speckle. In fact, it would be uncharacteristic behaviour for any police officer. 'What was nicked from the Lamplin house?'

'An antique diamond necklace and matching tiara and, as it turned out, five hundred quid which had not been reported initially but came out in the guv'nor's questioning. All very odd, wouldn't you say?'

'Anne!' PC Brian Scuttle's shout echoed along the narrow hall. 'Blower. Personal. Some bloke called Richard.'

'A mature man, eh?'

'Spendthrift brother. On the bum, I shouldn't wonder.'

Lukeson picked up a batch of photographs from the Murphy crime scene and went through them, pausing on seeing Bridie Murphy lying in a pool of her own blood. 'What a cruel end to a pathetic life,' he murmured, and promised: 'I'll not rest until I nail the bastard who did this to you, Bridie.' The photographs chronicled Bridie Murphy's miserable life, saddest of all, the streaks of blood on the uncovered floorboards that told how she had dragged herself across the room from near the room door, where the pattern of blood spatters on the wall showed that her killer had struck her down when she had opened the door to him. Her killer had clearly come with murder in mind.

The door opened and CS Frank 'Sermon' Doyle entered.

'Good morning, sir,' Lukeson greeted the Chief Super cheerily, though feeling far from cheery.

'About these murders, Lukeson. Any progress?'

'I've no doubt we'll get our man, sir.'

Doyle frowned. On hearing his words echo away, Andy Lukeson winced at how flippant they sounded to him. So how much more flippant must they have been to Doyle's ears.

'You are up to it, aren't you, Lukeson?' Doyle growled.

'I hope so, sir.'

'I've often thought that police work is like the Grand National. It's the promising ones that always come a cropper at Beecher's Brook.'

'If I haven't got your confidence, sir . . . '

'Don't be so bloody ready to throw in the towel, man,' he barked. 'If I didn't think you could nail the bastard who did this, you'd be out on your arse by now. All I ask of you and everyone else around here is that you be honest with me, rather than leaving a mountain of shit on my carpet for ACC Mulgrave to stir with the Chief Constable. Understood?'

'Perfectly, sir.'

He turned to leave. 'I'll need things to happen soon, Lukeson.'

'Sir.'

Frank Doyle paused in the open door to look at Andy Lukeson, the way a headmaster might at a student who had not proved worthy of the promise he had shown and the faith he had put in him. 'Soon, Lukeson,' he said, and departed.

There was no need for Doyle to elaborate on what it would mean if Lukeson did not meet his requirement of 'soon'.

14

'Lousy timing that, love,' PC Alan Walsh groaned, on seeing Anne Smith come to the window of the wholesale electrical store he had under observation, just as he was about to use the public loo a little way along the street which, strictly speaking he should not, in case the man he was looking for turned up. But the six pints of bitter he'd consumed at a friend's birthday party the previous night needed to be unloaded, and it was not his fault, due to budget restrictions, that he had no back-up. After all, what was he supposed to do, sit for two more hours with a full bladder.

The man at whom Smith cast a glance got into a ramshackle van and drove away.

Walsh let some distance build up between them before following. Ten minutes later, the van made a right turn into a street he knew as Cranway Street, a street that was well past its Victorian glory days, but having something of a renaissance, with some of the ramshackle houses making the transition from cheap rental accommodation back to Victorian elegance.

Walsh slowed, glancing about as if looking for an address, conscious of being easily spotted in the narrow, traffic-free street.

★   ★   ★

A PC came forward to meet Sally Speckle and Charlie Johnson when they arrived at the Lamplin house. Rupert Lamplin was speaking agitatedly to a second constable, who was trying to calm him down.

'She's in the garage, ma'am,' the PC informed Speckle, who hurried ahead. The constable cast an appreciative glance after Speckle. 'What's it like to have a bird for a guv'nor, Charlie? Especially one who's the stuff of wet dreams.'

'OK, Len.'

'Wouldn't fancy having a bird as my boss.'

'You're married, Len. You have a bird as your boss.'

'Oh, very funny.'

'What happened here?'

'Mrs Lamplin came from the house, there's a door from the kitchen into the garage, to open the garage door for her old man. He'd phoned ahead. He reversed in. She waited in the garage to direct him in, as normal, because with junk on either side it's a tight fit. Anyway, the accelerator stuck, and before

Lamplin could take any action his missus was part of the plaster on the back wall of the garage.'

'Nasty.'

'The poor bastard's cut up badly.'

'I expect he would be. Better join the boss.'

Len Brown sighed. 'Wouldn't mind getting in her knickers.'

'Your old woman would serve you up for dinner.' DC Charlie Johnson walked away laughing.

★   ★   ★

Walsh had a moment's panic when he could not see the red van, and was relieved that he hadn't cocked up when the man he was following stepped from behind a high-sided removal truck half-way along the street, having parked ahead of it.

He pulled in. Then cursed, when his sudden movement to the kerb attracted the man's attention. He paused to look along the street. Walsh acted smartly. He got from the car and walked a short distance back along the street to an empty house. He paused. Stepped back. Looked up at the house. Made a show of checking a blank piece of paper from his pocket, as if checking the address. He went up the steps, resisting the urge to glance back along the street until he reached the front door. 'Shit,' he swore. Not only had the man's interest in him been maintained, but he was walking towards him.

★   ★   ★

'You can check with the garage,' Rupert Lamplin was saying to Sally Speckle when Johnson joined her. 'I had booked my car in for attention to the accelerator. It was sticking.' He held his head in his hands and moaned. 'God, I should have taken the replacement car they offered to loan me. But I hate getting the hang of driving a strange car.' Johnson looked into the garage where a blanket covered Cecily Lamplin's body, the blood seeping through. 'Poor dear, sweet Cecily.' Lamplin staggered back, clutching at his right leg. Johnson prevented him falling.

'Are you all right?' Speckle enquired.

'Not really, Inspector. As I explained to you, I had polio as a young man and since then stress affects the muscles of my right leg. Makes it go suddenly numb and awkward. I feel rather unwell. I think I should go inside and summon my doctor.'

'Of course,' Speckle said.

'You're most kind and understanding, Inspector,' he said. 'Thank you for coming to my assistance, officer.'

'Not at all, sir,' Johnson replied.

Lamplin looked back into the garage, and repeated, 'Poor dear, sweet Cecily.'

★   ★   ★

'Buying, are you?' Walsh turned as if startled by the man's voice. He looked up at the house and pulled a face. 'Bit of a mess. But with a bit of TLC it would come up as bright as a new penny, like the one I'm doing the electrics in along the street. Should have seen that six weeks ago. This place is a bloody palace compared.'

'Seems a lot to take on,' Walsh said, in a tone of voice that showed appreciation of the man's interest and advice.

'Worth it, though,' he opined, 'when you see the finished product. Me and my mates could — '

'Oh, I'll give it some thought.'

'Yeah.'

The man's loss of interest was instant when he did not see ready cash in the offing.

'But if you give me your name and telephone number,' PC Alan Walsh said. 'I'll give you a call if I decide to go ahead.'

The man's interest was quickly rekindled. 'Starkie. Andrew Starkie. I'll jot down my phone number, shall I?'

'Thanks.'

'Me mates and me will do you a good deal.'

Until I slam the front door shut and the house comes down round me, Walsh thought. Starkie walked off. Walsh noted the house he turned into. Then, chuffed with his first outing in civvies, which should edge him closer to being a detective in CID, his ultimate goal, he phoned Andy Lukeson.

★ ★ ★

'Well?' Charlie Johnson quizzed Speckle as soon as Lamplin was out of earshot. 'Do you believe that load of old tosh?'

'Tosh?

'He's done for her. Plain as the nose on your face.'

'By what circuitous cerebral route did you arrive at that conclusion, Charlie? Lamplin loved his wife.' A great deal, she thought, to have put up with her free-love lifestyle. But, of course, Johnson had not been privy to her private chat with Lamplin.

Johnson squared up to his superior. 'What went on between Lamplin and you in his study, guv?' he demanded to know bluntly.

Speckle struggled with her promise of confidentiality to Lamplin, and her duty as a police officer to share information. It had been foolish to agree to Lamplin's request for absolute confidentiality to begin with. However, that assurance was given in good faith at the time. But now, if Charlie Johnson's suspicions about Cecily Lamplin's death had any substance, then surely that pact of confidentiality went out the window. But where Johnson seemed to have no doubt about dirty dealing afoot, she, on the other hand, had no difficulty in accepting Rupert Lamplin's version of events. He had said that he had been in contact with his garage about the sticking accelerator, information that was instantly checkable. He was no fool. He would not have spun such a blatantly cock-and-bull yarn which could be easily checked. An examination of the car would quickly verify if the accelerator was faulty. However, if Lamplin was no fool, that could equally mean that he was a very clever killer who had set up a very plausible scheme of murder?

'If you're not prepared to say, ma'am, I'll walk right in there and ask him,' Johnson said starkly.

'That's a threat to a senior officer, DC Johnson,' Speckle said. 'And this senior officer doesn't like being threatened.'

'I say something smells in all of this,

ma'am,' Johnson said, holding his ground. 'And I reckon that as a police officer, irrespective of how my senior officer thinks about it, I have a duty to unearth any wrongdoing. What went on between you and Lamplin is police business, ma'am.'

The stand-off was short lived.

'You're right, of course, Charlie,' she agreed. 'So I'd best tell you what happened in that study. If for no other reason than for my reputation's sake.'

★ ★ ★

'Fourth house along, sir,' Walsh informed Andy Lukeson when he arrived. 'Name's Andrew Starkie.'

'Good work,' Lukeson complimented.

'Thank you, sir,' Walsh said eagerly, casting a smile Helen Rochester's way. He was of a mind to make a pitch for a current detective constable's vacancy in CID, but decided that a quiet word later might be more fruitful. A DI's (even an Acting DI's) recommendation would carry a lot of weight. And Lukeson was acknowledged as one of Loston CID's finest coppers. The vacancy for a DC which he had in mind was on DI Jack Porter's team which, it was said round the nick, would be Acting DI Andy Lukeson's team before long more.

'DS Rochester and I will take it from here. You report back to the station.'

'Back to the ... yes, sir,' Walsh said politely, but stiffly. His face said: *Bloody typical. I do all the work and you take all the credit!* For a moment Rochester seemed of a mind to intervene.

'Walsh is a good copper. Should have a good future.'

'You reckon?' Rochester said enthusiastically, before realizing how she had let her guard down.

'If he can curb his impatience.' Lukeson smiled. 'You might have a word, Helen.'

'Me? Have a word,' she said innocently, but dropped her pretence on seeing Andy Lukeson's look. 'Yeah. He is a bit of an eager beaver, isn't he.'

'Weren't we all,' Lukeson said. 'I know I was sure that within a year of joining my full potential would be realized and they'd beg me to become Chief Constable.'

Rochester laughed. 'Me, too.'

'Walsh could slot in nicely I reckon to that DC's vacancy on my ... Porter's team.'

'Word is, it'll be your team shortly, Andy.'

'No counting of chickens until they hatch, eh.'

He drove past the house in question, parked further along the street near a lane that gave access to the rear of the terrace. 'You take the back,' he told Rochester. 'I'll go in the front door.'

'As befitting a DI, I reckon,' Helen Rochester chirped. 'DS round to the tradesmen's entrance, thank you very much.'

'Take care, Helen,' Lukeson said concernedly. 'Remember, trapped animals are dangerous.'

★   ★   ★

'Bloody Moses!' was DC Charlie Johnson's reaction to DI Sally Speckle's briefing on Cecily Lamplin's sexual escapades. 'That's a pretty strong motive for murder, don't you think?'

She could not deny that it was.

'But why now, Charlie? Lamplin's put up with his wife's eccentricities for years.'

'Eccentricities? That's a nice word for screwing round.'

'Why, out of the blue, would he up and top her?'

'The pot finally came to the boil?' Johnson proposed. 'He had to be simmering all these years. If he wasn't, it wouldn't be natural, would it. So he had enough. Only so much a man can take, guv. I'd have topped her years ago.'

'He could have left, Charlie.'

'Leaving would start questions being asked, questions that might bring it all out in the open. He'd not want that. Make him look a right prat.'

Speckle recognized the logic of Johnson's reasoning. Offended male ego and pride were often the precursor to trouble. Fear of his wife's secret lifestyle becoming known had been Lamplin's primary concern when he had spoken to her. So what if the urge to murder had come because the man who had come to the Lamplin house had returned to the goose with the golden egg and had threatened to make public her indiscretions if his demands were not met? Blackmailers sucked their victims dry. And there was always the threat that they would eventually disclose the secrets of their victims or, if apprehended, would do so out of malice. Apprehended, there would also be a court case in which every aspect of Cecily Lamplin's life would be gone into. So would it not be the blackmailer whom Lamplin would kill?

Or . . .

A thought as black as Satan's soul came to Speckle's mind. Perhaps, to be certain that he was rid of all complications, Rupert Lamplin had killed them both to keep the secret and to rid himself of a double burden? As things now stood, he would be a grieving saint instead of a vicious killer.

Speckle sat back in the driver's seat of the Punto and sighed wearily.

'New man in your life wearing you out, is he, boss?' Johnson asked with a cheeky grin.

'For the benefit of the grapevine in Loston nick, the new man in my life, as you put it was, and I stress *was*, my boyfriend a long time ago, but is now simply my house guest. Not that my personal life is any of your damn business, DC Johnson. And that goes for the entire nick. So put the word out, eh.'

'Must have plenty of dosh.'

'Meaning?' Speckle asked sharply.

'None of my business, guv.'

'Meaning?' Speckle insisted.

'Lorenzo's isn't a chippie, is it.'

'A win on a horse.'

'That hoary old chestnut,' Johnson scoffed. 'Must have used that one a hundred times meself.' When Speckle glared at him, he held his hands up. 'Only looking out for my senior officer's welfare, like a good team player should.'

'Give me patience,' she said. 'I've got to swing round by my place to pick up a report I was working on, and forgot to bring with me.'

A hoary old chestnut.

As she drove away from the Lamplin house, DI Sally Speckle's mind was on Johnson's reference to Simon Ambrose's sudden riches. And she finally had to admit to herself that she had never really believed the story about winning on a horse. Because Simon never used to gamble. 'It's a mug's game.' His own words.

So if he had not won on a horse, where did he get the money? Of course, he could have changed his view on gambling in ten years.

She hoped.

★ ★ ★

'Police,' Andy Lukeson said to the man who finally opened the door of the house. The sound of a drill, muted when the door had been closed, became ear-shattering. 'Looking for Andrew Starkie.'

A man up a ladder further along the hall, working on a fuse box, jumped to the ground and ran along the hall to the rear of the house. Lukeson gave chase. A door opened outwards to impede him. A man came from a downstairs toilet zipping up, and did a funny little jig with Lukeson as he tried to get past. Starkie had bolted into the kitchen, well ahead of Lukeson. Just as he reached the kitchen door it was yanked open to reveal

238

Helen Rochester. 'Andrew Starkie, I presume,' she said.

'Piss off!'

'OK.'

Rochester slammed the door in Starkie's face, enjoying the thump of wood on bone. The collision catapulted Starkie back across the kitchen into Andy Lukeson's arms. 'Nice one, Helen.' Before Starkie gathered his senses, Lukeson marched him along the hall.

'What am I suppose to have done?' he demanded to know.

'You've come under suspicion for stalking a woman by the name of Anne Smith,' Lukeson informed him. 'And perhaps a great deal more.'

'Don't know no Anne Smith,' he said surlily.

'All will come out in the wash, Starkie.'

'And what's this great deal more, eh?'

'All in good time,' Andy Lukeson said. 'All in good time.'

'Who's goin' to do the electrics then,' the man who had come from the toilet complained.

15

'Coffee?' DI Sally Speckle invited Charlie Johnson. 'Don't mind if . . . no, I'll take the sun,' he said, changing his mind about accepting his guv'nor's invitation on spotting a man, presumably Speckle's house guest, at an upstairs window. He leaned back in the passenger seat. 'Won't be able to afford Lanzarotte this year, I reckon.'

'It's midwinter, Charlie.'

'Yeah. But the sun through the windscreen is nice.'

'Please yourself. Won't be long.' Turning to go inside, she saw the edge of a bedroom curtain fall into place, and immediately knew the reason for Johnson's change of mind.

Simon Ambrose was coming downstairs. Speckle's gaze settled on the scruffy holdall he was carrying, the only luggage he had come with. 'Thought I'd hit the road, Sal,' he said. She had returned unexpectedly, so that meant that he had intended to slip away when she was absent and be gone when she arrived home.

'A bit sudden, isn't it, Simon?'

'Time, really. And admit it, you'll be glad to be rid of me.'

She did not deny his assertion. 'Where are you headed for?'

'Here and there.'

'Don't you have an address where I could contact you?'

'You won't want to contact me, Sally. I'm a ghost from the past, best left in the past.'

'Simon, where did you get the money to take me to Lorenzo's?' she enquired, deciding that it was time to confront Ambrose and either sweep aside any doubts or, alternatively, to confirm what had been her growing suspicions, with all that that entailed, should they be well founded. It was a question she hated to have to ask, but the police officer in her, and perhaps the woman too, would not let her rest until she did.

'Lorenzo's. Where did that come from?'

'Answer the question, Simon. Please.'

'God, I wouldn't have thought it possible. Carefree, there's always tomorrow Sally Speckle, one hundred per cent copper.'

'A bet, you said?'

'Yes. That's what I said.'

'Name of the horse. Time and location of the race.'

Her mobile rang.

'Lousy timing,' Ambrose said, continuing to the front door.

'Yes, sir,' she answered. 'Haven't decided

yet. Probably an accident, but Lamplin could have set the whole thing up.' Speckle wished that CS Frank Doyle would hang up, because when she had mentioned the name Lamplin, she had noted the halt in Simon Ambrose's step. 'Something's come up. Can I phone you back, sir?' She broke the connection before Doyle could agree or disagree.

Simon Ambrose had the front door open. Speckle, the woman, wanted him to leave. However, Speckle the police officer had one more question to ask.

'Might that horse be called Lamplin's Folly, Simon? Cecily Lamplin's folly to be precise?' He turned and looked at her steadily, but did not answer. 'Simon, if I looked in your holdall, would I find an antique diamond tiara and necklace? And if I searched your pockets would I find what's left of five hundred pounds?'

There was no need for him to reply. His downcast appearance did that for him, much to Sally Speckle's hurt.

'You mentioned Cecily Lamplin just now. An accident?'

'Jury's out.'

'What happened?'

'When Lamplin came home, his wife opened the garage door for him to let him reverse in. The accelerator on his car stuck, and before she could get out of the way she was smashed against the back wall of the garage.'

'Plausible. But I'd have my doubts if that's the way it was.'

'Why, Simon?'

'Cecily Lamplin was terrified of her husband.'

'That's not the impression I got.'

'Believe me, she was, Sally.'

'Did she say why she was terrified of him?'

'She mentioned a dark secret.'

'Hers or his?'

'At the time I couldn't have cared less. I was already planning to make our dalliance work to my advantage.' He grinned sadly. 'Your face is a picture, Sally. Yes, I'm a long way from the man you thought I was.' He placed the holdall on the hall table and unzipped it. He unrolled a vest to reveal the Lamplin jewellery. 'All that's left of the money is thirty quid.' He took a twenty and a ten-pound note from his pocket and placed them with the jewellery. 'Don't be so quick to condemn,' he said. 'Try spending every day living from hand to mouth. It's not easy.'

'But — '

'How did it come to this? When Sharon Lesley moved on and turfed me out, it was a shock. I stupidly thought that I was the love of her life, you see. It wasn't easy for me to accept that all I'd been was another conquest that she had tired of. It doesn't take long to slide down the ladder, Sally. One wrong decision, that's all it takes.'

He looked at the diamond tiara and necklace.

'I was planning a whole new beginning with that lot.'

'I'll have to — '

'Of course you will. You're a copper, Sally. Oh, don't worry. Banged up for the winter will be better than trying to find a charitable soul to take me in. I've turned into a regular bum, Sally. When I met you, I thought I'd struck gold. That maybe I could turn things round,' he said plaintively. 'Go back to the way things were. But that really only happens in Hollywood movies, eh.'

The pity about it all, Speckle thought, was that maybe, if . . . she cut short her thoughts. She went to the front door, opened it, and beckoned DC Charlie Johnson inside.

16

Andy Lukeson switched on the tape machine in Interview Room 4. 'The time is 1.16 p.m. This interview concerns the alleged stalking of Ms Anne Smith by Mr Andrew Starkie — '

'I never did no stalkin'.' Starkie barked.

'That was Mr Starkie denying the allegations,' Lukeson said.

'Too bloody right!'

'Present are Acting DI Andy Lukeson. Acting DS Helen Rochester — '

'Acting this, Acting that,' Starkie scoffed. 'What's this then, a drama school?'

'And Mr Andrew Starkie. Mr Starkie has been cautioned and advised that he may have his solicitor present. Mr Starkie's response was stuff it, copper. He was then advised that if he did not have his own solicitor, a solicitor would be appointed to represent him, to which Mr Starkie replied. 'Piss off'. PC Robert Chapps is also present.'

Lukeson sat back in his chair.

'Why have you come to reside in Loston, Mr Starkie?'

'Why not come to live in Loston?'

'Pure coincidence that Ms Smith happens

to now live in Loston, is it?'

'Don't know no Ms Smith.'

'I think you do, Starkie,' Lukeson said in a more determined tone of voice. 'And I think you followed her to Loston from Birmingham where, a year ago, you made a nuisance of yourself to Anne Smith.'

'Like I said, I don't know no Anne Smith.'

'Is it not a fact that you stalked Anne Smith?'

'Why would I do that then?'

'Fancied her, did you?'

'Couldn't have. Don't know her.'

'You have a history, Mr Starkie,' Helen Rochester said. 'Assault with a deadly weapon, namely a hammer.'

Lukeson could not help wonder about a possible connection with Bridie Murphy, who had suffered blunt trauma.

'I was fifteen years old. Just a high-spirited kid.'

'Fred Clarence was the man's name.'

'Don't remember. And I was never charged. The complaint was withdrawn.'

'Wonder why that was? Maybe it had something to do with Mr Clarence almost falling out of his apartment window.'

Starkie snorted. 'A long way down.'

'You'd know,' Rochester said. 'You were there.'

'Prove that, can ya?' He scoffed. 'Don't think so.'

'There's also the complaint by a Ms Julie Ashton — '

'A nutter, she was. Forty and never been opened, know what I mean, darlin'.'

'Like feeling female bottoms in pubs, do you, Mr Starkie?'

'Look, she gave me the come-on. Jiggling it all over the place like, she was. She was a teaser. Silly cow. I told her. I said, you could land yourself in a lot of trouble advertisin' a sale and then shuttin' the store.'

'Made a bit of a nuisance of yourself, didn't you,' Lukeson said. 'You followed Julie Ashton home several times. From the pub. From the gym. From work.'

He tapped his forehead. 'Her story.'

'Another non-starter, when Ms Ashton, who had been very positive up to a point, withdrew her complaint, like Fred Clarence did. Suddenly unsure about the man's identity and not wanting to do an innocent man wrong.'

Smug, Andrew Starkie leaned back in his chair.

'Terrible. Being the victim of dodgy identification. I must have the worst luck in all of England, you reckon, Inspector? But it's good that people are honest enough to admit their mistakes, ain't it.'

'Luckily Julie Ashton hadn't a cat,' Rochester said. 'It might have ended up being pushed through her letter box, garrotted. Just like Anne Smith's cat was.'

'Now you've lost me completely.'

'Like being violent towards women, do you, Mr Starkie?' Lukeson asked.

'Me? Naw. But I've heard that some women get off on bein' slapped 'round. Strange creatures, women.'

'Where were you between 11 p.m. on the 6th and 1 a.m. on the 7th, Mr Starkie?' Lukeson questioned.

'In bed.'

'Alone?'

'Yeah. Look, I didn't have nothin' to do with that bird in the park, if that's what you're gettin' at.'

'Why would you think that?'

'I know coppers. If it don't fit, then you make it fit, don't ya.'

'Do you know a pub called the Coachman's Inn?' Rochester questioned.

'Never heard of it. Look, on the 6th I was home all evenin' watchin' the telly. Skint, I was.'

'What were you watching, Mr Starkie?'

'Nothin' in particular. You know how it is. You sit. After a while programmes come and go, don't they. And after a coupla hours you can't recall what you were watchin'. Unless, of course, it's footie. Like football, I do. Reckon we'll win the World Cup? I was scootin' around most of the time.'

'Scooting around?'

'Switchin' channels.'

'Maybe you could give us a flavour of what you watched?' Rochester suggested. 'Sport. Comedy. Drama. News, for example.'

'Yeah.'

'Yes what?'

'News. Yeah. I watched the news.'

'Channel?' Starkie shrugged. 'News channels have very specific introductions to their news, Mr Starkie.' He shrugged again. 'Anything interesting on?'

'The usual stuff. Murder and mayhem.'

'Pretty depressing, isn't it,' Rochester empathized.

'Yeah. Pretty depressing.'

'I mean the mess that that suicide bomber in Afghanistan made. All those innocent people slaughtered in that market-place.' Helen Rochester shivered.

'Yeah. Shockin'.'

Helen Rochester looked Andrew Starkie directly in the eye. 'There was no car bomb in Afghanistan, on the 6th, Mr Starkie.'

Starkie swallowed hard.

'Where were you, Starkie?' Lukeson rasped. Suddenly every smidgen of Starkie's cockiness vanished and he became a trapped, furtive animal. 'Don't be stupid enough to drop yourself in it more than you already have.'

'OK. I was outside Anne Smith's flat,' Starkie admitted. 'But I had nothin' to do with no murder.'

'If you're as lily white as you say you are, Starkie, why did you take off when I wanted a word?'

'Shit meself. Coppers have that effect, don't they.'

'It wouldn't be that coppers play a big part in your life, and whenever they turn up it means that they've rumbled you again?'

'No. It all comes from me childhood, you see. This big gorilla in blue tried to get his hand inside me trousers. To the present day I break out in a cold sweat. It's what the shrinks call a fear of authority figures thingy-me-bob. Can't think of the right word. All I know is that if you've got it, you go all jittery when something out of your past comes back.'

'Do you know a woman named Bridie Murphy, Starkie?' Lukeson asked.

'Irish,' he snorted contemptuously. 'I'd have nothin' to do with no Irish bird. And I think I'll have that solicitor now.'

Lukeson said, 'Interview suspended at 1.33 p.m.' He nodded to Chapps, who came forward. 'PC Chapps is escorting Mr Starkie to a remand cell until a duty solicitor can be contacted.'

When Starkie left, Rochester asked, 'How do you reckon Starkie for murder, Andy?'

'I don't,' Lukeson said.

'That's very positive.'

'Maybe I'm wrong, but I don't think Starkie has the kind of bottle it takes to commit murder. Unless it was a punch-up outside a boozer or a football match. Something of that nature.'

'He's a stalker, Andy. And he's not averse to violence.'

'I don't really hold with the idea that every stalker or loner is a killer, Helen. In fact, statistics prove that most murders are committed by family members or friends of the victim. Stalkers and loners are always good press. Sells newspapers, if they can include the words stalker or loner in the headline. But, just in case I'm talking through my rear end, get a warrant to search Starkie's flat.'

*   *   *

'Tell the copper investigating the murder in the park he should ask Nick Clark about it,' the woman on the phone told the WPC who took her call, in a hushed voice. 'Wouldn't put anything past him.'

'And where might we find this Nick Clark?'

'Got to go,' the woman said urgently.

'Wait!'

In the second before the woman hung up, WPC Granger heard another female voice in the background and smiled smugly, a smugness that held all the way to Interview Room 4 where Acting DI Andy Lukeson was, and who now responded:

'You are a clever copper. You're sure that's what you heard in the background?'

'Yes, sir. Clear as a bell. Top Hat Insurance.'

17

Reginald Hampton was nervous when he saw Andy Lukeson and Helen Rochester again, but he relaxed a little when Lukeson enquired about Nick Clark and he realized that it was not he they had come to see.

'Clark? He's the upcoming, Inspector.'

'The upcoming?'

'Yes. You'll recall that Ms Blake had been recommended for promotion by her upcoming section manager. And I explained that upcoming was — '

'Decided, but not yet appointed, something like that, wasn't it?'

'Yes, that's right.'

'So Clark would have a say in Kate Blake's career path?' Rochester queried.

'Yes. Decidedly so.'

'What kind of a man is Mr Clark?'

'I'm not sure I understand your question, Inspector,' Hampton hedged.

'Oh, I think you do, Mr Hampton. So what kind of a man is Clark?'

'You're placing me in a very difficult position, Inspector,' Hampton complained.

'Not nearly as difficult as Ms Blake found

herself in,' Lukeson said tersely.

'There have been one or two rumours. But probably nothing more than office gossip, I shouldn't wonder.'

'Indulge me, sir,' Lukeson said.

'Let's just say that rumour has it that Clark brings certain pressures to bear.'

'On female staff in his section?'

'Like I said — '

'Office gossip.'

'All . . . ' Hampton gave up the ghost. 'I'll have you know that I was opposed to Clark's advancement, Inspector.'

'Did Clark try it on with Kate Blake?'

'I can't say. Like I told you, my involvement with Ms Blake was fleeting and very foolish.' He gave a short little laugh. 'If you're asking me was I jealous, Inspector, my answer is, not in the least.'

'What about angry?'

'Angry? Why should I be angry?'

'Perhaps because Clark took something from you that you wanted to keep?'

'That's utter nonsense!'

Andy Lukeson studied Hampton, who cringed under his scrutiny. 'I'd like to speak to Mr Clark now.'

'Not possible. He's off sick.'

'Since when?'

Hampton became thoughtful. 'Well, actually

since the morning after Ka . . . Ms Blake was . . . ' He shook his head vigorously. 'No, I can't believe that Nick had anything to do with her death. A bit of a lad with the ladies, he might be. But a murderer . . . ?' He shook his head again.

'We'll need Mr Clark's home address.'

'It's company policy not to divulge — '

'Mr Hampton,' Lukeson cut in sharply. 'We need Mr Clark's address, and we need it right now.'

'Yes. I understand.' He went to his desktop computer and typed in. He then scribbled on a piece of paper, brought it back and handed it to Andy Lukeson.

'Now, there was a phone call made to the police from here at 1.28 p.m. this afternoon.'

'Was there? What about?'

'Presumably you keep a record of all calls made, Mr Hampton?'

'Yes, we do.'

'And can you trace those calls?'

'Yes. Once an outside line is used, details of the extension are recorded. Telephone bills can be a major part of expenditure, so — '

'And are extensions specific to a desk or an employee?'

'In the main.'

'Good. That will save us a great deal of time, Mr Hampton. We'd like to speak to the woman who made that call. Will it take long? Time is of the essence,' Lukeson said, when it looked like Hampton might go into dither mode.

'Of course. I'll see to it. I'll have a word with our Mr Phillips. He looks after things technical round here.'

'Thank you.'

★ ★ ★

CS Frank Doyle laid aside Sally Speckle's report about Cecily Lamplin's death with the comment: 'A bit indecisive, wouldn't you say? Seems to me that it was an accident, plain and simple. You've checked with the garage, of course?'

'Yes. They've confirmed that Lamplin had booked his car in to have the accelerator checked. And, as you know, sir, the lab have confirmed that the accelerator cable was frayed. Only a couple of strands of cable.'

'Enough to cause it to stick?'

'Most of the time, but not all of the time.'

'Percentages, Speckle.'

'Ten tests. Six snags.'

'More or less shouts accident, doesn't it?'

'I agree, sir, but — '

'Put before a jury,' Doyle interjected. 'There would be a strong, a very strong case indeed,' he emphasized, 'of reasonable doubt, if it's

256

murder you're asking to convict on. Agreed?'

Sally Speckle nodded.

'So an unfortunate accident it is, then?' DI Sally Speckle's hesitation irked Doyle. 'Look, it's my opinion that the Crown Prosecution Service wouldn't go near court on a murder charge.'

Frank 'Sermon' Doyle's eyes bored into her, willing her to agree.

'Lamplin could have doctored the cable himself, sir. I imagine that, using pliers or a hacksaw, it would be easy to undo a couple of strands of wire. Or possibly a bit of effort with something like sandpaper to fray a couple of strands — '

'Cuts and fraying are detectable,' Doyle pointed out. 'And even if some signs of interference were found, could proof positive be brought forward to a court of law? A clever defence could easily cast doubt and sway a jury, Speckle. And Lamplin did talk to his garage about this sticking accelerator cable.'

'Lamplin might be a very clever killer setting the scene, sir.'

Doyle sighed.

'He might indeed. But can you prove it, Speckle?'

Sally Speckle's answer was an indecisive shrug.

'Even if this was a very clever murder, which frankly I don't believe it was, with what we've got we haven't a dicky bird's chance of convincing judge and jury. That's the bottom line. Defence would call specialist witnesses, and you know how impressed with specialist witnesses juries can be, to state cables wear all the time. It was just unfortunate that on this occasion it had not been attended to as promptly as it should have been, unfortunate, but not intentionally criminal. If Lamplin did murder his wife, the uncertainty that could be planted in a jury's mind would have him walking from court, Sally.'

'Lamplin might have a motive for murder, sir.'

Doyle frowned. 'And what might that be, Inspector?'

Speckle told him about Cecily Lamplin's unusual lifestyle. 'It was a man she picked up who came to the house and was *given* the jewellery and money that was reported as being stolen, sir.'

'Have I been on some bloody distant planet of the Martian solar system not to have heard all this before now, Speckle,' he berated her.

'It was a work in progress, sir.'

'Don't give me that load of old rubbish, Inspector! You've been keeping secrets, haven't you?'

'There is something else.'

'Oh?'

'It's about my house guest, sir.'

'Your house guest, Speckle?' Doyle enquired, bewildered. He sat back, looking at a very troubled Sally Speckle. 'Well, go on then.' Ten minutes later, ten minutes that were the most difficult and humiliating in Sally Speckle's life, he said, 'Let me sum this up. This Simon Ambrose, former boyfriend — '

'A long time ago, sir.'

' — and your present house guest, was the man who blackmailed Cecily Lamplin, and tried to pick up the woman who was murdered in Layman's Park. And was, on the night, wearing a yellow scarf which could be the murder weapon used in her murder?'

'In a nutshell, sir,' Speckle responded quietly.

'Some bloody nutshell, Inspector!'

Doyle could already see the newspaper headlines:

FUGITIVE FINDS REFUGE AS POLICE INSPECTOR'S GUEST.

Once the ferrets of the press, particularly the gutter press, got to work it would not take long for them to discover Speckle's former relationship with Ambrose, and even though it was a long time ago, the link between past and present would be mercilessly used to sensationalize the story. There would be lots of stories about bad apples in the barrel needing to be rooted out. Politicians needing a cause to either hang on to their parliamentary seat, or those who had ambition (and they all had, mostly beyond their abilities) would latch on like leeches to fresh flesh. There would be those within and without who would use Speckle's downfall to bad-mouth the Graduate Entrance Programme. The old argument about traditional ways versus new ways would be resurrected with gusto and no small amount of invective, the end result of which would be ground lost that would take an age to regain at a time when police concentration should be focused on dealing with the increasing lawlessness in society. Situations like this made officers senior and junior more cautious because of the *I could be next* syndrome which would be set in train, the end result of which would be a handsome bonus for the criminal fraternity. Defence counsel would not be shy either to raise all sorts of issues of trust to get their clients off the hook. Frank Doyle was of the opinion that the uncovering of possible corruption within the police had an even greater detrimental effect than a miscarriage of justice — that was often categorized as a mistake — but corruption was in-house and all corrosive. It created a *them and us* climate of fear and mistrust that in the long run did no one any good. Although more a traditionalist than new wave, as he had been once described by a colleague, Doyle recognized in an increasingly sophisticated world of criminality, that more was needed than a gut feeling, a notebook and a stub of pencil.

'A bit of a mess, this, Speckle,' he grunted. 'A friend, eh. How good a friend?'

'You mean were we at it like rabbits!'

Frank 'Sermon' Doyle faced down Speckle's defiant outburst. 'You're in enough trouble without taking me on, Inspector,' he said. 'You got yourself into this, so you've only yourself to blame. Full disclosure is demanded and needed.'

'Simon Ambrose was my guest and nothing more, sir.'

'In your opinion, is this fellow Ambrose capable of murder?'

'Is my opinion worth anything right now?'

'Frankly, from Joe Public's point of view, little or nothing. But I'd still like to have it, Sally.'

'I don't think so, sir. But such an assertion has to be seen in two ways.'

261

'Which are?'

'That I was at one time very much in love with Simon Ambrose and, honestly, might have been again. And, of course, there is always the rose-tinted glasses danger after a gap of ten years.'

'You'll have to keep a low profile.'

'I'm not given to skulking, sir,' Speckle said. She placed her warrant card on the desk. 'You'll be needing this.'

'Not yet. Maybe never.' He handed her back the warrant card. 'This has a long way yet to run to the finishing line. But I'll be up front with you. I've seen shit on fans before, but never in this quantity, this thick, or with such a stickability factor. Does Lukeson know?'

'I've been trying to get hold of him, but his mobile is powered off.'

'What's the point in having a mobile if it's powered off!'

'Andy doesn't like to have his train of thought interrupted by a bleeping phone. As soon as I can I'll — '

'Leave it to me,' Doyle said.

Sally Speckle thought: already outside the circle.

Although he had tried to remove some of the black from the picture, Frank Doyle could see only one outcome to all of this — the end of Sally Speckle's career.

18

'Nice,' Helen Rochester observed, on turning into the leafy lane four miles from Loston, where Nick Clark's house was situated. As it turned out 'Happy Hollow' was the last house at the end of the lane. Turning into the driveway, one would reasonably take the house to be unoccupied, had Lukeson not noticed the edge of a downstairs curtain falling back in to place.

Five minutes later, and several hammerings with the brass knocker and as many peals of the doorbell chimes, Lukeson's patience was spent, so he went and knocked on the downstairs window. 'Police. You're not helping yourself by pretending you're not at home, Mr Clark,' he called out. 'Now, I can ask the questions I need to ask you from out here, or you can be sensible and let us in.' A moment, and the front door opened. A man in a dressing gown, unkempt, stubbled and bleary-eyed put in an appearance. 'Inspector Lukeson. Sergeant Rochester.'

'I had nothing to do with Kate Blake's murder,' he blurted out, gripped by panic.

Either their arrival and the subject matter

had been announced by Reginald Hampton, or Clark was expecting them to turn up. For a second, before he stepped aside to let them enter, Lukeson thought Clark was going to slam the door. He led the way along the hall to the kitchen at the rear. It was a gloomy house, lots of rooms as in houses of the period, but no real room. Therefore when he reached the kitchen, which was bright and cheery and very spacious (obviously several smaller rooms knocked into one), he was pleasantly surprised. Wisps of steam were coming from the electric kettle on the worktop near the sink. A mug with a spoon in a bowl of sugar and a jar of instant coffee were next to the kettle.

'I was just about to make a cup of coffee. Care to join me?' Clark invited.

'No, thank you,' Lukeson refused curtly.

Clark was on edge, and that's the way he wanted to keep him. Any social element to the visit might relax him, and the appearance of the big bad wolf might be diminished. Rochester understood Lukeson's reason for refusing, but did he have to include her. She'd give anything for a cup of coffee and one of the iced buns in a newly opened packet, and to hell with her present diet. She could always work a couple of hundred calories off. Feeling pangs deep in her tummy, she remained steadfast at Lukeson's side, the faithful underling, thinking that sometimes the life of a police officer made demands that were above and beyond mere human endurance.

Andy Lukeson came straight to the point.

'If, as you claim, you had nothing to do with Kate Blake's murder, Mr Clark, why are you hiding out like a hunted fugitive? Why didn't you come forward to help the police with their inquiries?'

'I was hoping you'd catch her killer and that would be the end of that. My fake bout of flu would be over, I'd go back to work, and everything would go on as before. I'm not proud of myself, Inspector. I've been very foolish, haven't I.'

If he was hoping for sympathy from Lukeson, it was in short supply.

Clark sipped his coffee to ease the croak in his voice. 'My wife doesn't need to know about all of this, does she? Luckily, she's visiting her sister in Oxford at present. All of this bother would upset her no end, I'm sure.'

I'm sure, too, Helen Rochester thought. What a pathetic sack for any woman to be remotely interested in. 'Did you coerce Kate Blake to accompany you to the Coachman's Inn, Mr Clark?'

'Coerce? I have no need to coerce any

woman, Sergeant,' he said petulantly.

'Is that because, as a section manager, you hold sway over their future?'

'How dare you!'

'This is a murder inquiry, Mr Clark,' Lukeson said, in response to his outburst. 'All sorts of questions must be asked, and answered,' he finished pointedly.

Clark snorted. 'You've been talking to Sylvia Crane, haven't you? Sour grapes, I'm afraid.'

'Would it be correct to say that when you take a fancy, you are not above applying pressure to get women to concede to your wishes?'

'Don't you have any control over your junior?' Clark enquired hotly of Andy Lukeson. 'Kate Blake was ambitious.'

'So it was a situation of you scratch my back and I'll scratch yours, eh?'

'Something like that.'

'Isn't it a pity that Ms Blake is not here to agree with or to contradict your opinion, Mr Clark.'

'I should never have taken the silly woman out in the first place.'

'As a married man, there is a case for that point of view,' Rochester said.

If looks could kill, Rochester thought.

'There was a dispute involving another

man who took advantage while you were — '

'Nothing but a bit of pub nonsense, Inspector.'

'That's not how our witness described it.' Clark looked sullenly at Lukeson. 'Being left behind like that must have made you angry.'

'Left behind,' Clark ranted. 'I chose to remain behind, Inspector.'

'Perhaps even angry enough to follow Ms Blake — '

'Why would I do that?'

'To sort her out, maybe,' Rochester said.

'Kate Blake wasn't worth the bother,' Clark said dispassionately. 'I went back inside the pub.'

'A crowded pub, from which it would be easy to go missing for five or ten minutes?' Clark slammed the cup of coffee down on the kitchen table, sending the coffee and the shattered cup all over the kitchen floor. 'You do have a temper, don't you, Mr Clark,' Andy Lukeson observed.

Helen Rochester's mobile rang. She went into the hall to answer it.

'We'll need a full statement, of course,' Lukeson said.

'I've told you all I know.'

'We'll still need a full statement.'

'I'm ill,' Clark protested.

'No you're not,' Lukeson said, his mood

uncompromising. 'You're skiving off work, hoping that out of sight you'll be out of mind until all this blows over.'

Rochester came back into the kitchen. 'Yes, sir,' she was saying. 'I'll tell him.' She beckoned to Lukeson to follow her into the hall. 'That was CS Doyle on the blower, Andy.'

'I gathered that. To tell me what?'

'To leave your mobile on.'

'What's so urgent?'

'A short time ago, Sally Speckle arrested a man for theft and blackmail and on suspicion of murder.' Before she completed the content of Doyle's phone call, Andy Lukeson instinctively knew what was coming next. 'Kate Blake's murder.' What he could not figure out was how Speckle had become involved in a case that was not hers to become involved with in the first place.

'He's the second man in the argument outside the Coachman's Inn. The one wearing a yellow scarf.'

'Go on,' he urged with a sinking feeling.

'This man was Sally Speckle's house guest.' If a bolt of lightning had struck him, Lukeson could not have been more immobilized. 'One more bit of bad news, Andy. The lab has confirmed that the thread found snagged on a bush at the crime scene matches a wool thread found on the collar of this man's overcoat.'

★ ★ ★

Sally Speckle looked up when Andy Lukeson entered her office, her face a misery. His heart went out to her. On returning to the station, the news about Jack Porter's decision to call it quits would normally have been headline news but, regrettably, Speckle's problems (except for the odd couple of gloaters who always crept out of the woodwork when someone was in it) had taken precedence over all else. 'The shit's really hit the fan this time, Andy,' she said disconsolately. 'Harbouring a fugitive is serious stuff.'

'You didn't harbour a fugitive, Sally. All you're guilty of is having a house guest who turned out to be a bad lot.'

'Very charitable. But the newspapers won't be as charitable, Andy. They'll smell blood, copper blood, and you know the system. To placate the baying press hounds, a sacrifice will have to be offered up. And that'll be me.'

'Doyle won't wear that.'

'Frank Doyle will do as he's told, Andy,' she sighed. 'He's an old-fashioned copper, who thinks of the force first and foremost. If I

269

resign it will be easier all round.'

'Don't judge him, Sally. I reckon he'll be in your corner.'

'Oh, I'm not sure I want this any more,' she said wearily. 'Irregular hours. Any time off is very likely interrupted. Budget cuts that make it nearly impossible to do the job. Pay that comes no way near what I could earn in the private sector. And rubbing shoulders with people you wouldn't have in the doghouse.' She laughed sadly. 'We must all have holes in the head, Andy.'

Lukeson was stumped.

'Enough about me. You'll want to talk to Simon Ambrose.'

'Why do you think he might be involved in murder?'

'He may not be, but there's enough circumstantial to raise eyebrows. He was in the Coachman's Inn on the night of the murder. He tried to pick up the murdered woman. And she was strangled, probably with a scarf. There was a yellow wool thread found snagged on a bush at the scene, and Simon had a yellow wool scarf which he no longer has, and which he claims was stolen. And he was late getting home. After the time frame of the murder, which I understand to be between 11 p.m. and 1 a.m.'

'It might not be as black as it looks, Sally.

Bridie Murphy, the prostitute who witnessed the argument outside the pub, said that when she looked back there was a scarf on the ground. Now, what if Kate Blake's killer witnessed the argument, saw her going off on her own, grabbed an opportunity, retrieved the scarf, followed her, and strangled her with it?

Speckle shook her head doubtfully.

'Bridie Murphy said that she knew the *identity* of the man who followed Kate Blake. How could she have known your house guest, Sally? He'd have just been a man she'd seen in a dust-up outside a pub.'

Speckle's sigh was long and weary.

'Because he might have picked her up, Andy. Simon was very drunk. He says he wandered about. Having already tried to pick up Kate Blake proves that he was . . . well, up for sex. With anyone, by the look of it.' Lukeson's heart went out to Speckle as deep hurt masked her face. 'Isn't it possible, then, that drunk, blood up, if Bridie Murphy was hanging around he'd pick her up? Drunks talk, Andy.'

'But that means that Ambrose might have — '

'Assaulted Murphy, also? A right old mess, isn't it.'

'I'd better have a word with Ambrose, eh.'

Before beginning the Ambrose interview, Andy Lukeson went outside to get some fresh air and to get his head round the idea that Sally Speckle might not be around for much longer. He had quit smoking three years previously, but now more than ever since then, he was near to relapsing. Passing through Custody, a waif was sitting using her crayons to colour a colouring book while a couple argued at the Custody Sergeant's desk about who did what to whom. Feeling sorry for the little girl, he paused to admire her colouring.

'That's very good,' he said, looking at the face of a clown she had coloured in.

'No it isn't,' she groaned.

'I think it is,' Lukeson said.

'His hair should be black, not green.'

'Oh, I don't know. I like green hair,' he said, looking sideways at the clown.

'No,' she said positively. 'Black.'

She vigorously used a black crayon to change the clown's hair, ending up with a clown who had mostly black hair, but with green stripes running through it.

'Now that's really something,' Lukeson said.

The little girl giggled. 'You're silly.'

Andy Lukeson laughed with her. 'A lot of people say that.'

The little girl shook her head, and repeated, 'Silly.'

After a couple of minutes, Helen Rochester joined him outside. 'Something interesting popped up on that check you asked me to do on cold cases, Andy, the ones where something might have been taken from them. Three years ago there was a woman murdered in a park in London. She'd been wearing an ankle chain that went missing.'

Lukeson murmured, 'Kate Blake, an earring. Sandra Fairweather, a bracelet. And the woman in London, an ankle chain. What was her name?'

'Angela Lambourne. Trophies?' Rochester wondered.

'Maybe. And this fellow Ambrose seems to like jewellery. He still had it, when he might have tried to unload it. Perhaps he just likes things that glitter, Helen. How was Lambourne killed?'

'Strangled. And the scene was devoid of trace evidence, too.'

'It would be interesting to find out if someone among the people we've interviewed was in London at that time, Helen. And in the vicinity of Brigham when Sandra Fairweather was killed. And in Loston now.'

19

Simon Ambrose was a man defeated. He sat waiting, watched over by a PC who, although he was smaller in stature than Ambrose, towered over the slumped, shoulders hunched figure. When Lukeson entered Interview Room 2, he looked at Lukeson with a sad, disinterested resignation, and the intense hopelessness which one might experience when told by a doctor that nothing could be done. It would appear that Simon Ambrose had at last given up on a life that had proved too much of a burden to bear.

Lukeson went through the interview routine for the benefit of the tape before beginning a task he wished he could have avoided. Ambrose, being a thief and a blackmailer only, Sally Speckle might weather the coming storm, a storm through which he would support her through thick and thin. However, if Ambrose was a killer, Speckle would most assuredly have to resign. And even if by some miracle she was not called on to do so, knowing her, she would resign anyway, because as a police officer her reputation would have been irretrievably damaged. Every case she would take on after that, some hack would re-run her involvement with Ambrose.

Sally Speckle was too proud a woman to live her professional life under a cloud of suspicion.

'Tell me about what happened in the Coachman's Inn, Mr Ambrose,' Lukeson began.

'It's all in my statement,' he replied, showing no interest.

Though understandable, Ambrose's total capitulation angered Andy Lukeson. He hated quitters. 'Answer the question,' he barked.

Lukeson's attitude brought a spark of defiance to Simon Ambrose's eyes, but it was a weak flame that withered as quickly as it had flourished. 'In a nutshell,' he said mechanically, 'I was more than half drunk. She was sitting there — '

'She? For the benefit of the tape would you please indicate who she is?'

'The woman who was murdered in the park, of course. Isn't that what all this nonsense is about?'

'Nonsense?' Lukeson snapped. 'Murder is not some silly party game, Ambrose. A woman is dead. And someone took her life away from her.'

'It wasn't me,' Ambrose said quietly in defeat.

'Then if you're innocent of murder, it's all the more important for you to answer the questions put to you to enable us to find the real killer.'

'How is Sally?' he asked. 'Me hanging around has really dropped her in it. And that's the last thing I'd have wanted.'

'DI Speckle is in . . . let's say, an official quagmire because of you,' Lukeson said. 'And if you want to help her, then stop arsing about and get on with it! Now, the woman was sitting there . . . ?'

He looked at a point beyond Lukeson. 'A little earlier I had seen her arguing with this other man. As it later transpired, he was the man with whom she had arrived. He'd gone to the loo. So I thought that if I moved quickly, I might steal his crumpet.'

'How chivalrous of you,' Lukeson said, deadpan.

Simon Ambrose held Lukeson's hostile glare. 'Inspector, when you spend most days wondering where your next meal is coming from, and every night searching for somewhere to kip, you become less than choosy, and cunning and devious, and all sorts of things that you never suspected you were capable of or would ever become.'

'I'm not going to cry any tears. You were at Uni with Sally Speckle. How — '

'How?' he interjected. 'How did I become a despicable shite, Inspector? Pride, perhaps. Or more probably delusion. You see, I was to become the great writer. All I had to do was put the words on paper and publishers would beat a path to my door with the most incredible offers that would have me rolling in dosh. Awards would flood in. More dosh. I'd be fêted on telly, radio, press and the better end of the magazine market, nothing slushy. Oh, no. Definitely nothing downmarket. After all, I was a Nobel winner in the making,' he said with the intense bitterness of one whose disappointment was utter and total. 'By now I'd have so much dosh that governments would be asking me for a handout. *Sir* Simon was only a matter of the Palace recognizing my worth.

'Then, with the speed of a runaway train, I discovered the rejection slip. And soon, instead of publishers and agents beating a path to my door, there was only, yet again, the postman's footsteps and the ego-shattering clunk of another rejected manuscript on the hall floor with its by now very familiar slip telling me that it was good, but not quite their kind of thing.

'Soon, I was on the failure's classic route.

I'd have a drink to ease my angst with these idiots who could not recognize genius. At first I was convinced that it was only a matter of time. A publisher, a clever publisher, would accept my work and those other idiots would spend the remainder of their lives steeped in regret.

'But the more rejection, the more alcohol; the more disappointment, the more alcohol. Nothing makes a slope more slippery than whisky neat, Inspector,' he finished plaintively.

'The man with whom the woman arrived. How long did he stay after going back inside the pub?' Lukeson asked.

Simon Ambrose hunched his shoulders.

'Odd, wouldn't you say, Ambrose. You had tried to pick up his girlfriend. Had argued with him. I'd have thought that you'd feel the need to watch your back. Keep an eye on him all the time. These jealous disputes and alcohol are not a good mix. Liable to flair up again.'

'It was a chock-a-block pub. What could he possibly do.'

'At what time did you leave?'

'Closing time.'

'How long was that after Kate Blake departed?'

'An hour, give or take.'

'You never left the Coachman's Inn, in that time?'

'No.'

'Can anyone verify that?'

'I doubt it.'

'So you might have left the pub?'

'Presumably to commit murder.'

'Did you?' Lukeson asked. 'Commit murder?'

'I did not.'

Lukeson watched Ambrose closely. 'Meet anyone when you left?'

'Anyone? Such as?'

'A prostitute.'

'I don't frequent the species, Inspector.'

'The Coachman's Inn is a haunt for prostitutes, Ambrose. So how could you be sure that the woman you tried to pick up was not a prostitute? It might seem to a neutral observer that you were not as choosy on the night as your dismissal of the idea of picking up a prostitute suggests.'

'Having overheard some of her conversation with her companion, she was more the services for advancement kind, rather than a cash in hand woman, Inspector.'

'How could Sally ever have had anything to do with a man like you!'

Ambrose smiled slyly. 'Sally, Inspector? Has Cupid slung his arrow?' he sneered.

'Look, this woman was a very sexual woman, who was made even more sexual by alcohol. Any one of the hundred men in the Coachman's Inn might have . . . '

He held Lukeson's gaze.

'Haven't you ever been in a crowded pub and tried it on, Inspector?'

Lukeson was conscious of Helen Rochester's eyes on him. 'I'll ask the questions,' he snapped, quickly realizing that his reaction had answered the question in the positive. 'I put it to you that you can't say that the woman's escort was in the Coachman's Inn after she'd left, because you were not there yourself. That you followed and strangled — '

'I got sloshed. Left at closing time. Wandered about, and finally found my way back to Sally Speckle's.'

'Did it make you angry that the woman rejected you?'

Simon Ambrose snorted. 'If I murdered every woman who rejected me in the last couple of years, Inspector, half the women in England would have been strangled.'

'Did you see anyone else leave the pub soon after the woman departed?'

'People come and go all the time in pubs. Who takes notice?' From experience, it was a valid point, Lukeson had to concede. 'Of one thing I am certain. I did not.'

'Do you know a woman called Bridie Murphy?'

'No.'

'Ever down London way, Mr Ambrose?'

'A time or two, yes.'

'When were you there last?'

'It's hard to say.'

'Try to recall.'

'A couple of years ago, I suppose.'

Could that be three? Lukeson wondered. 'And Brigham?'

'Never been there.'

'Sure?'

'Certain, Inspector.'

'Found your yellow scarf yet?'

'No. The bastard who stole it is unlikely to return it.'

The interview, like all interviews until the all important one, ran out of steam. He could not see how he could progress it any further at that point, so Lukeson brought it to an end. 'Interview suspended at 3.41 p.m.'

'What now?' Ambrose enquired.

'We'll talk again, Mr Ambrose,' Lukeson said. 'Meanwhile, there are serious charges to answer.'

On leaving the interview room, in the hall outside, DC Charlie Johnson seemed to be doing an impression of Long John Silver, hobbling about on his left leg while dragging his right, much to the amusement of two PCs whose laughter died on seeing a grim-faced Andy Lukeson coming from Interview Room 2, realizing that they were probably looking at Jack Porter's replacement. His back to Lukeson, Johnson had not seen him and was oblivious to the body language of the PCs. 'Blasted damn coppers,' Johnson bellowed in a tony voice. 'Have you all flogged until your backs are raw.'

'What's going on here?' Lukeson questioned.

'Just my little joke,' Johnson said.

'And who are you supposed to be?'

'A fellow by the name of Rupert Lamplin. The boss and I interviewed him about — '

'I know all about it,' Lukeson interjected. 'Go and find something more useful to do!'

'I was on my way to see you, sir,' said the younger of the PCs. 'Someone slung a brick over the car park fence and it's smashed your windscreen.'

Lukeson groaned. When he turned to go back along the hall to reach the back stairs to the car park, the PC said, 'You'll have to go the long way round through Custody, sir. The doorlock at the end of the back stairs has packed in. Stuck.'

None too pleased, Andy Lukeson changed direction. It was, as it turned out, a most fortunate change.

★ ★ ★

On reaching Custody, the little girl he had spoken to earlier was still there and still colouring her colouring book. The woman was at the Custody Sergeant's desk answering questions which indicated that the man who'd been with her had been taken into custody.

'Nice giraffe,' Andy told the little girl. 'First time I've seen an orange giraffe, though.'

'Shall I give him black hair, too?'

'Might go well with the rest of him,' Lukeson said, after due consideration.

'OK, then.'

The crayon was used furiously, while Andy Lukeson looked on and watched the giraffe's black head take shape, becoming thoughtful, and more thoughtful.

20

'Do that thing again, Charlie!' Johnson, startled by Andy Lukeson's sudden appearance at his desk, was even more startled when Lukeson grabbed him and stood him up. 'The thingy you were doing in the hall with your right leg.'

'The Lamplin walk?'

'The Lamplin walk,' Lukeson said. 'Exactly!'

DC Charlie Johnson looked bewildered at WPC Anne Fenning and PC Brian Scuttle as Lukeson hurried from the room, not bothering to wait for the performance he had just requested from Johnson, muttering, 'Bookshop.' Twenty minutes later, Andy Lukeson found what he was looking for, a copy of Rupert Lamplin's latest book, the one Helen Rochester had posted to her aunt. 'Have you got a black pen of some sort,' he enquired of the female assistant.

'Felt do?'

'Lovely.'

The woman handed over a felt pen. 'Hair,' Lukeson said and, to her's and Helen Rochester's astonishment, he used the pen to vandalize the photograph of Lamplin on the dust jacket. The assistant looked along the counter to a man who was watching with increasing unease. 'Hair!' Lukeson said again, and showed Rochester the new image of Rupert Lamplin which she instantly recognized.

'That's the man who was with Bridie Murphy at the Coachman's Inn,' she said. 'Lamplin was wearing a toupee!'

'And I'm betting that the reason for the swept crime scene was The Lamplin walk, Helen.'

'The what?'

'Wait a minute!' the man along the counter hailed, when Lukeson went to leave.

'Police,' Lukeson informed him.

'You'll have to pay for this,' he said, picking up Rupert Lamplin's book. 'You've ruined it.'

'Cough up, Helen,' Lukeson said.

'Me?' she protested.

Lukeson left, leaving Rochester with no alternative but to put cash in the man's hand, which was uncompromisingly held out to her.

★   ★   ★

When the cleaning lady showed Lukeson and Rochester into the study, Rupert Lamplin set aside the whisky he was sipping. 'New troops,' he said lightly.

'DI Lukeson and DS Rochester.'

'All of this is becoming rather tiresome, Inspector.'

'All of this?' Rochester queried.

'The accident, of course.'

'We've not come about that,' Lukeson said.

'No? Then what have you come about?'

'Murder,' Lukeson stated bluntly.

'Murder? Who's murder?'

'A woman called Kate Blake.'

Lamplin cast his eyes upwards. 'Blake? You've lost me, Inspector.'

'Kate Blake is the name of the woman whom I believe you murdered in Layman's Park, Lamplin.'

'You're absolutely insane, man. I must ask you to leave my house this instant! And I shall be making a complaint, of that you can be certain, Inspector.'

Lukeson and Lamplin stared each other down. Lamplin was first to avert his gaze.

'There's also the murder of Sandra Fairweather in Cobley Wood, and a woman in London called Angela Lambourne three years ago to be taken into consideration. And the attempted murder of one Bridie Murphy, the woman you were with in the Coachman's Inn the morning after the Blake murder, when my sergeant and I were there.

'Ms Murphy knows the identity of Blake's

killer. She was about to tell me when she lapsed into coma. But I'll have that name when she comes to. And I believe that she'll name you, Lamplin.'

'This is utter nonsense,' Lamplin protested vehemently, but there was no denying he was rattled.

'Sergeant, would you please show Mr Lamplin his latest book,' Lukeson said.

'My latest book. What on earth . . . ? Rupert Lamplin paled on seeing his altered image.

Andy Lukeson took a paper from his pocket. 'This is a search warrant. I'm sure that along with the toupee you were wearing, we'll also find several items of jewellery taken from the murdered women, Lamplin: an earring from Blake, an ankle chain from Lambourne, and a bracelet from Fairweather. A search party will be here shortly.'

Rupert Lamplin was an animal trapped. His right leg began to tremble.

'A stressful situation, this. Leg acting up now, is it, sir? Like it does in times of excitement or stress since you got polio. That's the drawback with being a public figure. There's all that information on you out there. That's why you had to sweep the soft soil in Layman's Park after killing Kate Blake. Your impaired walk would have left evidence of a very distinctive departure from the crime scene, wouldn't it?

'I'm also confident that with a little effort we'll find that you were in London on the day Angela Lambourne was murdered. And also in the Brigham area when Sandra Fairweather was killed. So much traceable information stored in one form or another nowadays.' Lukeson allowed Lamplin a long spell of consideration, before saying: 'There really is no way out of this, Lamplin. Best to do it all quietly and avoid all the public rumpus, don't you think?'

A sudden resignation came over Rupert Lamplin.

'Cecily threatened to break our agreement,' he said. 'Couldn't live with our little secrets any more, she said, after finding another trinket, that drunken slut's earring. I suppose,' he said reflectively, 'that if there was an unravelling of our agreement, it was at that point when Cecily very foolishly, in a fit of pique, reported a false burglary. She was rattled when it went wrong, you see, and your Inspector Speckle called. And,' he slapped his by now shaking right leg, 'as I well know, once the jitters start, it's damn difficult to stop them.

'You'll find the trinkets in my safe, Inspector. Oh, and the murder weapons too.

288

Kept them all. A piece of twine, Lambourne. The belt of Fairweather's coat. The yellow wool scarf I used to strangle Blake.' He snorted. 'There it was on the street, as if it was meant to be, Inspector. An omen, wouldn't you say. The hammer I struck Murphy with you'll find in a skip, near Murphy's flat, where I slung it when passing.'

'Did you also murder your wife, Mr Lamplin?' Lukeson asked.

'Of course. But unlike the other killings, I took no pleasure in Cecily's demise. Her murder was simply a matter of self-preservation, Inspector. Whereas, the other women . . . ' His eyes shone insanely. 'Their own fault, isn't it, women I mean. Jiggling about. Damn teasers, the lot of them!' Ice broken, he went on apace. 'It really all started on my honeymoon. Excited, the leg acted up. Said that it felt like there was a snake under the bedclothes, Cecily said. Cruel, that. But then women are cruel creatures, aren't they.

'Soon afterwards, she admitted that she'd picked up a man on a bus, of all places, and had sex with him; sex from which she was still glowing three hours later. Obviously her addiction had begun. I did not want the scandal of divorce and all the public ballyhoo that that would bring. So I put up with her antics for years. Then one day, a hot July day in London, I was there for a book signing, I went for a walk in a park and saw Angela Lambourne walking ahead of me, her buttocks jiggling up and down in her tight jeans. At first, nothing much happened, but over five minutes or so, the demon I had worked so hard to keep locked up got free. I strangled her. And it was then that I found my addiction, Inspector. We all have them, don't we. It's just that most of us never become aware of them. But once the genie is out of the bottle . . . well, all is lost.'

He looked Lukeson steadily in the eye.

'I murdered Angela Lambourne, Sandra Fairweather and Kate Blake, Inspector,' Lamplin confessed. 'And, I suppose, Bridie Murphy too. But somehow, I think that death will be a release for her.' He laughed with the intensity of a madman. 'Gave me quite a start when you said she was in a coma, Inspector. Must have a thick skull, eh.'

His laughter became manic. His gaze fixed on some distant place from which Lukeson reckoned Rupert Lamplin would not be returning from any time soon, if at all.

Andy Lukeson arrested and cautioned Rupert Lamplin, but it did not matter. Nothing could reach him where he was.

'He'll never stand trial, will he?' Rochester asked as Lamplin was driven away.

Lukeson shook his head. 'Fast-tracked to the loonie bin, I shouldn't wonder. You know, if he'd toughed it out . . . '

'You didn't have a search warrant, Andy.'

'A good bluff is a valuable tool in a copper's chest of tricks, Helen,' he said.

'And,' she grinned impishly, 'a good bluff needs a good bluffer to make it convincing. Well done, DI Lukeson.'

Andy Lukeson grinned. 'I couldn't have done it without you, DS Rochester.'

★   ★   ★

When he called, a neighbour told Lukeson that she had seen Sally Speckle leave in a cab. 'Looked like she was going away for a spell,' she said.

'Did she say where to?' he enquired hopefully.

'No. Kept herself to herself,' she said, a little critically. 'All over the newspapers. That man she had in the house. Awful, isn't it. And her a police officer, too.'

Lukeson walked away. Having acted before being compelled, Sally Speckle had absented herself. He wondered if he'd ever again see her. Or if she would ever again want to see him.

Walking away, his mobile rang. He listened

for the second it took to tell him that Bridie Murphy had passed away. At least, he thought, she'll be back in Tipperary now.

His mobile rang again.

'Taking Porter's job, are you, Andy?' Frank 'Sermon' Doyle asked.

He broke the connection and powered the phone off. To hell with everyone!

We do hope that you have enjoyed reading this large print book.

Did you know that all of our titles are available for purchase?

We publish a wide range of high quality large print books including:
**Romances, Mysteries, Classics
General Fiction
Non Fiction and Westerns**

Special interest titles available in large print are:
**The Little Oxford Dictionary
Music Book
Song Book
Hymn Book
Service Book**

Also available from us courtesy of Oxford University Press:
**Young Readers' Dictionary
(large print edition)
Young Readers' Thesaurus
(large print edition)**

For further information or a free brochure, please contact us at:
**Ulverscroft Large Print Books Ltd.,
The Green, Bradgate Road, Anstey,
Leicester, LE7 7FU, England.
Tel:** (00 44) 0116 236 4325
Fax: (00 44) 0116 234 0205

Other titles published by
The House of Ulverscroft:

FOUL DEATH

J. A. O'Brien

DI Sally Speckle gets a phone call from a man who calls himself Fred telling her that he has left a birthday present for her at the Old Mill. The call makes no sense, but it unnerves her, particularly as the call is from a payphone in Loston Mental Hospital. Her present is the battered body of a faceless young woman. Then there is a second body and Speckle and her team realise they are dealing with a possible serial killer. Who will keep a cool head and save Fred's next victim, unmask the killer and solve the case?

REMAINS FOUND

J. A. O'Brien

Two children find a woman's body which is identified first by a friend called Ruby Cox, as Diane Shaft, and later by another friend, Aiden Brooks, as Cecily Staunton. Why did the dead woman have two names? DI Sally Speckle's problems start when Cox vanishes from Loston police station. Then Brooks, claiming he's a clairvoyant, accurately pinpoints the location of where the body was discovered. Does this mean that Brooks is the killer? But as the investigation gets increasingly complicated by troubles far closer to home, followed by another murder, Sally finds she has more suspects than she wants . . .

OLD BONES

J. A. O'Brien

When skeletal remains of a female are found in Thatcher's Lot, Loston CID is involved and DI Sally Speckle and her team investigate. The remains have been in the ground for five years — disturbingly, there were several women who went missing around that time. The missing women come from divergent backgrounds, but the skull has evidence of expensive dental care which Sally hopes will help to identify the remains. However, due to DC Helen Rochester's astuteness, the other women come into focus and unlikely suspects emerge. Now it starts to become a murder investigation within a murder investigation . . .

PICK UP

J. A. O'Brien

Jack Carver is experiencing the most horrible of all nightmares: being an innocent man who is the prime suspect in the brutal murder of two women. Forensic evidence is found at both crime scenes, which implicates Carver. And when the police request that he should come forward, he goes on the run instead. He is finally apprehended, but an incident from Carver's past shakes his absolute certainty that he is not the killer. Then he is charged with murder. Can DS Andy Lukeson prove his innocence when a chance incident prompts him to reassess the case?

LOVE TO DEATH

Patti Battison

What happens when love goes bad — and it becomes an obsession . . . ? Ageing rocker Johnny Lee Rogers is performing a series of charity concerts in Larchborough. His biggest fan, librarian Lizzie Thornton, has won tickets to see his final show. She's convinced that Fate is bringing them together . . . and Lizzie's always wanted a December wedding. As the town basks in the hottest temperatures for decades, it will be no Summer of Love for DCI Paul Wells and his team. Lizzie, a group of travellers and a missing girl seem to have conspired to bring a time of torment, intrigue and murder.